OUTSIDE IN

OUTSIDE IN

IN

Sarah Ellis

Groundwood Books
House of Anansi Press
Toronto   Berkeley

Groundwood Books / House of Anansi Press
110 Spadina Avenue, Suite 801, Toronto, Ontario M5V 2K4
or c/o Publishers Group West
1700 Fourth Street, Berkeley, CA 94710

We acknowledge for their financial support of our publishing program the Canada Council for the Arts, the Government of Canada through the Canada Book Fund (CBF) and the Ontario Arts Council.

 Canada Council Conseil des Arts
for the Arts du Canada

 ONTARIO ARTS COUNCIL
CONSEIL DES ARTS DE L'ONTARIO

Library and Archives Canada Cataloguing in Publication
Ellis, Sarah, author
Outside in / Sarah Ellis.
Issued in print and electronic formats.
ISBN 978-1-55498-367-4 (bound). — ISBN 978-1-55498-369-8 (html)
I. Title.
PS8559.L57O98 2014   jC813'.54   C2013-905605-X
C2013-905606-8

Cover illustration by Michael Cho
Design by Michael Solomon

Groundwood Books is committed to protecting our natural environment.
As part of our efforts, the interior of this book is printed on paper that contains 100% post-consumer recycled fibers, is acid-free and is processed chlorine-free.

Printed and bound in Canada

FSC
www.fsc.org
MIX
Paper from
responsible sources
FSC® C016245

For Cole, Julia and Grace

ONE
Honey Jar Jump

"Sweet color of the sound of you …"

Crash!

Lynn pulled the music out of her ears. What was going on downstairs? Was Clive building something?

She squinted at her phone. 9:37. Early on a Sunday, even for Mr. DIY.

Voices pushed into the room, Shakti and Clive, not the words but the anger of it, the unmistakable final chorus of a full-blown fight. It wasn't unusual to hear her mother at triple forte, but Lynn had never heard Clive that loud.

She glanced at the crowded bookshelf.

"What's going on, Kapok?" Kapok the bear came alive briefly and shrugged.

The bedroom door rattled as the pressure in the house changed. Somebody had left. Lynn slid out of bed and peered through her blinds.

Clive. The top of his head. Three giant steps and he was in the car.

What? He didn't walk around and do the circle check? Clive *always* checked for stray cats and toddlers on tricycles. Not this time. He peeled into the road and was gone.

The tinny sound of Synesthesia escaped from under the duvet. Kapok remained in a state of inert plush.

Lynn rubbed her eyes. It was way too early to tune in to a new Shakti drama.

≈ ≈ ≈

"CLIVE WILL BE back. He needs time to process. He and I are just at different stages on our journey — "

Lynn grabbed the nearest thing, a battered copy of *Affirmations for Wholeness*, and slammed it down on the table. Plates rattled. The jar of honey danced toward the table's edge, threatening suicide.

"Why don't you just take every good thing in your life and flush it down the toilet?"

Shakti leaned across the strewn newspaper and sticky crumbs, reaching for Lynn's hand. She had the eager, sparky look that she got during big juicy emotional scenes.

"Oh, Sixer, I hear that you're angry. Isn't it good to express it? Share what you're feeling."

Sixer was the nickname from Brownie days. Shakti had thought it was so cute that Lynn wanted to join Brownies, a paramilitary, post-colonial organization that propped up the patriarchy or some such thing. Lynn had just liked the uniform and the badges and the reliable tidiness of it all. She had liked being a sixer. Calling Lynn Sixer was a peace offering.

Thought balloon: *You are so full of crap*.

No. She was not going to share.

Lynn screeched her chair back, stood up, grabbed her jacket and pack and headed toward the door.

"Lynn. Wait. Where are you going?"

Thought balloon: *To score some dangerous drugs and have unprotected sex with a stranger*.

"Library. Homework."

≈ ≈ ≈

LYNN'S FAVORITE study carrel was free. She sat down, emptied some random objects out of her pack to establish territory and turned to stare out the window.

Had Shakti's revelation been a surprise? No. Things added up. Or, rather, things that didn't add up became clear.

There were those strange phone hang-ups and last-minute cancellations of plans because one of Shakti's friends was having a crisis. It seemed like every week she was all over some new thing. Since when did Shakti care about Bosnian hip-hop? There was the three-day skills-upgrade workshop, the workshop that Shakti said she took that weekend of the transit strike. Somehow she made it across three municipalities to get there. Lynn remembered Clive at the dinner table. "But there *weren't* any buses."

And Shakti doing her flirty thing: "Oh, don't be tiresomely literal."

Then there was the barbecue with the staff from the extended-care home where Shakti worked, the barbecue where, as it turned out, the whole thing started. Did Lynn remember some nurse's husband named Brandon? No. What she remembered was how her mom was that day — wound up, a little crazy, like a preschooler on top of a sandpile, legs apart, air-punching, the king of the castle.

In the car on the way home that day, Shakti got more and more jangly, her hands whipping up the air, as the back of Clive's head got more and more frozen. Lynn remembered telling herself that it was okay, that Shakti was just happy and wasn't that better than angry or flat?

And, finally, the email. The email to Brandon (*Brandon*, stupid name) that Clive found this morning. Of course it was an email. Shakti always left yawning cupboards and clothes-erupting drawers in her wake. Why would she clean up her mailbox?

Lynn gnawed at a hangnail. A cup of coffee wafted by the carrel. She pivoted in the comfortable library chair and looked out the window. Was that gray smear of a cloud moving?

What if Clive had really gone? For good. What if it was just her and Shakti again? The past five years — the Clive years — had been so ordinary. Milk in the fridge, friends over to play, money for school trips, air without jangle, a mother you didn't have to read for signals of a meltdown.

They had lived at Clive's townhouse all that time, the longest they'd ever settled anywhere. Five years in one school. A clothing allowance. A bus pass. Cable. Picking a paint color for your room. Actual holidays where you went away in the car with a cooler and stayed in motels and, like, visited the dinosaur museum and you could take a friend and the parents of the friend were okay with that because Clive was so obviously the kind of person who did the circle check. And Shakti had taken a course and gotten a job and started to seem more normal. Lynn had let herself believe that her mom was the leopard who *could* change her spots.

Somewhere out of sight a little kid was singing a private three-note chant.

Before Clive. A memory came sneaking back. They were living in a house with other people. Was that the year of Geoff? Was that the house where the mean boy cut off one of Kapok's ears? Or was that another house? Shakti was sitting on a blue couch, the one that was good for jumping on. She was rocking and crying, crying with gulping. Flowers always made Shakti happy. There were flowers next door. Lynn went to pick them but just when she had a big bunch, the next-door man came into his yard and yelled at her. He had an ogre voice. Then Shakti came out and yelled at the man and there was too much scary yelling. What was the end of that story?

And then Clive came. All of Shakti's other boyfriends, you couldn't let yourself like them too much because they always left. Except for Clive. Except for maybe now.

A text message pinged her into the present.

It was Kas. She and Celia wondered where Lynn was.

Kas and Celia. The friends. Clive called them the Diode.

Lynn's need for them flowed right out of her fingertips. She needed to tell them.

≈ ≈ ≈

"But what happened?" Celia snugged her chair close to the study table.

At the prospect of putting it into plain words, Lynn felt grubby. "Oh, it's all completely reality TV. She's like somebody pulled out of the audience of some bad talk show. She's been having, like, an 'affair' with the husband of one of the nurses at work. He's young, just married. They have a new baby. The guy's name is Brandon."

"Brandon." Kas scowled. "What a douche."

Celia flinched. Lynn gave her an It's-okay look. Kas's range of insults had recently become more colorful, and Celia was obviously having a hard time keeping up. As usual, she took refuge in wide reading and statistics.

"But more than half of married couples have an affair over the course of their marriage. Most just put it behind them and move ahead, with the help of professional counselors."

Kas looked unconvinced. "Where did you read that?"

"Magazine at the orthodontist."

Lynn loved the Diode, but they didn't seem to be getting

it. The person to be mad at was not Brandon, who hardly seemed like a real person at all, but Shakti. Shakti with her stupid affirmations and that little blissed-out smile that she had adopted — a smile that just made you want to shake her, shake her back into the real world.

"Look. The point is not Brandon or married couples. The point is that Shakti has no intention of putting it behind her. She thinks Clive is just going to adjust."

"Wait. She's just going to go on with — "

"That's the idea. She thinks she'll just go on with Clive and add Brandon. She thinks it'll be …" What was that hideous Shakti word? "Enhanced."

"Get out." Kas shook her head.

"But …" Celia looked as though she hadn't ever read a magazine article about this situation. "What about Brandon's wife? Your mom works with her, right? Does she know?"

"Well, obviously not," said Kas, forgetting to use her library voice. "Oh, sorry, Lynn. I don't know. Does she?"

"No, but Shakti thinks Brandon should tell her because then somehow that will just fit into her plan of enhancement."

Kas shook her head. "Hardcore."

Lynn translated for Celia. "Yeah, bad. You know, I didn't even want to know about all this stuff. She just made me listen to it. You know what she's doing? She's showing off."

It fell out of Lynn's mouth before she knew she knew it. That was it. Shakti was that kid on the sandpile. Look at me! I'm being bad!

The Diode was silent. Kas pulled a bag of toffees out of her pack and passed them around.

Celia passed. "Braces. You know."

"*Celia.* Lynn is having a crisis here. The least you can do is eat a toffee."

For once, Celia ignored Kas's complete lack of logic. She grabbed one, ripped off its paper and stuffed it defiantly into her mouth.

"You're right. I *will.*"

Lynn followed suit. Werther's. The hard kind. The best.

Kas and Celia. They had adopted her that first day at her new school, a kid with a weird mom, a pretend-tough eight-year-old who had almost given up trying to make friends.

Kas cut to the chase. "Do you think Clive will come back?"

Lynn thought of the car reversing onto the road. Clive never bailed. Even during the Parent Advisory Council disaster, when Shakti got in some fight with the president and decided to sue and then had to quit her job because of stress and spent months sitting on the couch writing angry emails to all the parents and teachers, Clive hung in.

Until now.

The toffee was suddenly disgusting, that sweet-before-sick taste.

"He might not."

Kas cracked her toffee between her teeth. "Will he still be, like, your dad?"

Celia jumped in, a family lawyer in the making. "Of course he will. They were in a common-law relationship. There can be joint custody, child support, all kinds of different arrangements — "

Kas put her hand over Celia's. "Celia. Shut up."

"Oh. Right. Okay."

Lynn ejected the toffee back into its paper. "About Clive? I just don't know."

The opening notes of "Whistle" bubbled up from somewhere deep in Celia's backpack. She squinched up her face.

"Sorry. I'm due home. Piano practice."

"It's okay," said Lynn. "I need to go, too."

"Come on," said Kas. "We'll walk you."

They gathered their stuff. As they left the library, Kas tucked the bag of toffees into Lynn's jacket pocket.

TWO

Nearly Dying

THE WORLD SLIPPED out of alignment but Thursday still followed Wednesday and Socials followed Choir followed Math and there was always and forever homework.

The difference between mass and weight? Lynn and Kas decided to discuss this scintillating question at Lynn's place.

"What's with the claw?" said Kas, pointing to the dining-room ceiling, where an arrangement of naked metal and bare bulbs hung like some instrument of torture.

Lynn dumped her pack on the table and tossed her jacket over the back of the chair.

"It's her latest thing. Since Clive left she's cleaning and stuff, off and on. She took the crystals off the chandelier to wash them but that was two weeks ago."

"So. Is Clive still doing that condo-sit? Does he come around?"

"No." Lynn swallowed. "He phones. Me. Actually, he phoned this morning. He's going away. To Ghana."

"Ghana!"

"Yeah. His company was always trying to get him to go there, to lead some kind of training course. About micro-finance. He always said no before but now he said yes."

"For how long?"

"Three months."

"Three months. Wow. Major."

Lynn nodded. It was a black hole. Even when he came back, would he be back?

Kas upended her bag on the table and fished out a science textbook. "Hey. Do you hear dripping?"

Lynn listened. "Nope. We should start reviewing."

"Can I get a drink?"

"Sure. Get me one, too. I think there's some juice in the fridge."

Kas came back balancing two glasses of juice and a box of healthy corn cheese snacks.

"Your fridge has a sign that says that it's vibrating with energy and health."

"Oh, gack. They're everywhere. Affirmations. I go to floss my teeth and there it is on the bathroom mirror: I am my own unique self. What's the one on the remote? I express my needs and feelings. It's revolting."

Kas sighed and opened the science text. "Okay, let's be affirmative. We are going to ace the quiz tomorrow. Weight is a force. Mass is a … You know, I definitely hear something dripping."

"It's probably just the tap in the bathroom upstairs. You can't turn it off properly."

The tap was one of the many things that had gone wrong after Clive left. Lost keys, a weird smell under the kitchen sink, the fig tree in the living room that dropped all its leaves, a handful of cable channels that suddenly disappeared. It was starting to seem as if the inanimate world had only been held in place by his presence.

"So," said Kas. "Your weight on a scale is really just an estimate of mass. Huh? Hey! What about Alexis getting that solo instead of Celia?"

"Wrong. Capital R wrong. Celia's got a way better voice. I don't know why Mr. Inkpen picked Alexis."

"Hair."

"What?"

"Hair. When we go to Portland for Choirfest there's going to be all these American groups, right? Have you looked at them on YouTube? They've all got that big blonde hair, Glee hair. And uniforms. We're going to turn up in our white blouses and dark skirts, looking like nuns. We don't stand a chance against them. We need Alexis, her hair, the whole package. And she can belt it out."

"Yeah, she can belt it out but not on pitch or on the beat."

"Yeah. Well. Cele doesn't care. She wouldn't know how to hold a grudge."

Lynn inspected her day-glo orange fingertips. "Are these things stale or are they supposed to taste this way?"

"Back in a minute," said Kas, heading for the stairs. "Figure out Newtons while I'm gone."

Lynn had barely opened her notebook when there was a yelp.

"Help! It's all wet!"

Lynn bounded up the stairs. Kas was dancing around the hall, bouncing from one foot to the other.

"What happened?"

The first step into the hall and her feet sank into the soggy carpet.

Lynn pushed open the bathroom door. The sink was full to the brim, and a thin stream of water flowed down the cupboard. The floor was a shallow lake.

"Quick!" Lynn leaped toward the sink. Her foot slipped on the wet floor and she went down, bashing her knee on the side of the tub. She scrambled up, plunged her hand into the cold water of the sink, causing a small tsunami that beached itself down the front of her sweatshirt. She grabbed the plug and pulled.

Kas was still dancing on the threshold. "Are you okay? What should I do?"

"Grab some towels." Lynn pointed at the door of the linen cupboard.

The water glugged and slurped away, leaving a sodden shirt sitting in the sink.

Kas started pitching towels. Mop wring, mop wring. They pulled off their soggy socks and rolled up their pants. The bathroom floor was one thing, but the hall was a giant sponge. They spread towels on the carpet and walked on them but the wet kept rising.

Kas started to jump up and down to help squish out the water. "Weight and mass are our friends. But it's not working that great. What's that cloth thing they're always advertising on the Shopping Channel?"

"ShamWow. We so need that nutso hyper salesman guy."

In time, every absorbent thing was wet. Every bathmat, facecloth, ancient beach towel, every tea towel from the kitchen. Lynn stood and stared at the soggy mass piled in the bathtub and the shirt in the sink. She pulled off her sweatshirt and tossed it onto the pile.

"She's such an idiot."

They retreated down the still-soggy hall to Lynn's bedroom.

"What do you mean?" asked Kas.

Lynn's knee was throbbing and her fingers were pruney. She pulled on a sweater and then punched the bed.

"Everything's a mess. Last night she dropped pizza on her shirt. She must have put it in the sink to soak this morning. Of *course* she forgot about the drip. Since Clive left she's been totally out of it. I am so finished with her."

"Is that Brandon guy still, like, in the picture?"

"Yeah. Her latest thing is that I should meet him to 'normalize the situation.' Not. Going. To. Happen."

"Hardcore."

"Hey. Thanks for mopping up with me."

"Are you kidding? This was way better than reviewing

for science. When else would I get a chance to do such an all-in towel toss? But … do you still hear dripping?"

Lynn listened. She put her ear to the wall. The drip was definite and regular.

"Okay, this is ridiculous. She needs to deal." She pulled out her phone.

Nice Noreen was on the desk. "Oh, hi, Lynn. Your mom? Oh. But she's not … Um. She's not available at the moment. Sure, I'll take a message, but maybe you'd better try her cell, sweetie."

Lynn clicked off. "Weird. Nice Noreen sounded confused. And why try Shakti's cell? She doesn't have it on at work."

Lynn saw Kas glance at her watch.

"You have to go, right?"

"Yeah. Babysitting."

Lynn pivoted off the bed and rummaged in her bottom drawer. "Here you go. Dry socks. Least I can do."

≈ ≈ ≈

LYNN STOOD at the bus stop. Bus, bus, stay away. Come again some other life. Life at the end of this particular bus ride was life gone wrong.

She had quit. Shakti had quit her job. Things had gotten a little "awkward" with Brandon's wife and really it was a good opportunity because Shakti felt that it was time for a realignment of her energies and a reevaluation of her skills.

This was all revealed last night, right after Lynn discovered the spongy damp wall in the basement. Shouldn't

Shakti get somebody to fix it? Not to worry, she'd email Clive about it.

Lynn had to ask. Was Clive still in their lives and if not what were they doing living in his house? The answers were pure Shakti. Well, he was still being a bit "rigid" but he'd said that they could stay there for three months. And then? Then they'd have a wonderful opportunity to reimagine their lives. Lynn doubted that "wonderful opportunity" had been Clive's words.

At that point Shakti came clean about quitting. "Job, house, let's shake it up a bit!"

It was horribly familiar. Before Clive, Shakti bounced from job to job. She was very good at getting jobs. She charmed interviewers. She could always talk the talk. But after a short while there was always something wrong. The hours were bad, the commute was impossible, management were bullies, her coworkers didn't appreciate what she had to offer, the culture was toxic. So she would quit and then there wouldn't be rent money so they would have to look for a cheaper place.

Was it all starting again?

Lynn peered down the street. No bus. The guy with the parrot on his shoulder walked by. Some hyper kids pushed the Wait signal button about eighty times until a senior with a cane told them to knock it off. The woman with the free newspapers blessed everybody who took one.

The only good piece of timing lately was Choirfest in Portland. Mr. Inkpen was squishing in all kinds of extra rehearsals to get the choir in shape. Having to stay late after school was perfect. Lynn could hardly wait to get on that coach headed south across the border and leave Shakti and her mess behind.

Hsssss. A bus approached. Lynn looked up. Not in Service.

Right. Whatever. Every day after school she stared at the same crosswalk, the same skinny tree, the same mailbox, the same stores. *ClairVoyant: Registered Psychic* was closed, as usual. Perhaps Clair just knew when a customer was on the way.

No sign of another serviceable bus. Fine. The waiting crowd was getting bigger, and there were mild rumblings of complaint and the inevitable theories.

"They just don't return from the loop."

"I figure it's that construction tie-up by the bridge."

"Less bus. Every day, less bus. Is no good."

Lynn rubbed her itchy eyes. Nature was playing along with the theme of irritability by bringing into bloom some plant that activated her hay-fever button. She reached into her pocket for a tissue.

Crinkle? It was the bag of candies that Kas had given her. Werther's Original toffees. Now *there* was something you could count on.

When it was all over, the nearly dying that happened then, Lynn thought of all the potential hazards of the street. Drunk driver plows into bus stop. Stray bullet from gangland shoot-out. Metal fatigue causes shop awning collapse. Meteorite.

You don't think of a Werther's toffee and a black dog with big feet. You don't think of that combination.

She had just slipped the toffee into her mouth when the dog appeared, bouncing at the end of a long and saggy leash. It had a waving feathery tail, a dog grin and an owner weighed down with bags and parcels.

The minute it spied Lynn, it bounded over to her and jumped, jerking on its leash. Its big hard paws landed right on her boobs and it hurt like crazy and she gasped as the dog bounced off her.

Inside the gasp was the toffee.

The owner's parcels went flying. The dog did a joyful half-twist. The bus crowd started to react. Lynn tried to inhale.

There was a loud silence. Not one bit of air was getting in. Every part of her brain was screaming for her to cough but there was nothing, no sound, no air. Nobody was paying any attention to her, all busy with helping to gather up the dog lady's scattered parcels as the dog, now off leash, ran around in circles, barking.

From some survival file in her mind Lynn retrieved the sign for choking and put both hands up to her throat. Still, nobody was looking at her. Her brain started to buzz. She kicked the nearest person.

"What the …"

"Omygod, she's choking. Can you speak?"

"Get that damn dog out of the way."

"Help me here. Phone 911 somebody!"

"Muggins! Off!"

It seemed to go on for hours.

And then, one quiet voice behind her. "I'm going to help you. I'm just going to slip off your pack." She felt the pack slide off and two skinny arms encircled her, paused for a second and then, shockingly, squish-punched her in the middle.

The toffee shot out of her mouth and pinged off the mailbox.

One ping and that was it. Lynn doubled over and took one ragged, raspy breath and a second. Her chest and throat and head hurt but the lovely air just kept coming in and out.

Nearly dead and then not dead at all. She straightened up.

The bus people crowded around with questions and pats to her arms and offers of water. Muggins' owner was practically crying. Someone held out her pack. Muggins, now tied to a tree, seemed to be having a nap.

Lynn tried to find her voice. First there was just a froggy croak and then she pushed out one word. "Who?"

A woman in a shawl pointed down the street. "There she goes. That girl."

Lynn turned just in time to see a figure in a plaid kilt and knee socks disappear around the corner.

THREE

I Saw You

"Wow," SAID KAS. "Clive leaves, you find out that you might have to move, and then you nearly choke to death, all in the same month. That's a lot of stress." She skooched her plastic lounge chair along the pool deck to the table and leaned forward. The music for the Nifty Sixties Deepwater Aquasizers bounced off the pool walls.

"Yes," said Celia. "Must be well over a hundred points."

"Points?"

"Holmes and Rahe stress scale. For example, acquiring a physical deformity gives you eight times as many points as a family vacation."

"What do I get if I have more than a hundred points? HD TV? Cruise?"

"No, you get to be sick."

"Oh. Big whoop."

"The question is," said Celia, "who was she, that Heimlich girl?"

Lynn shrugged. "I don't have a clue."

Celia, using her flipflop as a gavel, pronounced, "There is *always* a clue. There is *always* evidence."

Lynn grinned. Celia was destined for law school. According to Celia, law school was what Korean parents thought good daughters should aspire to. Celia had an evidence-based approach to life.

Celia continued, "Think. Relive the moment. What do we have? A kilt. What does this suggest?"

"Exchange student from Scotland?" said Kas.

"Yeah," said Lynn. "On a bagpipe scholarship?"

"Do girls even play bagpipes? If not, why not?"

"Four! Three! Two! One! Good job, ladies!" The blond buffed-boy aquasize instructor danced on the deck. He never stopped moving, talking and teasing the nifty sixties. "Just one more rep, Marjorie, show us your stuff!"

Celia gave Kas and Lynn a look of judicial disdain. "We are straying from the point. I believe what you meant to say was private school. And what else? Distinguishing marks? Height? Hair color? Style? Sound of voice? Accent? Smell?"

"Um. A little taller than me. Her arms felt skinny. Brown hair, pulled back. I hardly saw her. Ordinary voice, not that I heard her say very much. Hang on … There was a smell. Dirt."

"Ick."

"No, not ick dirt. Like dirt-when-you-dig-in-the-garden dirt."

"Obviously the tartan is our strongest lead. Would you recognize it again?"

"Um, maybe. It was mostly green."

"Kas, your assignment is to research the uniforms of all local private schools."

"Okay, but here's a question. Why do we even want to find her?"

"Oh." Celia frowned. "I just assumed. Lynn?"

"I'd just like to know who she is. You know, to thank her. Otherwise I would always wonder."

"Okay," said Celia. "What other approaches can we take?"

"There's got to be something online," said Lynn. "How do people find other people?"

"I know!" said Kas. "I Saw You. In that free paper. Wait. There's a pile of them near the entrance."

She scooted off down the pool deck and was back in a minute. She spread the paper out on the table.

"Here it is. I Saw You. Have you looked at it before?"

"Yeah," said Lynn. "That paper's usually around the house."

"Um," said Celia, "I'm not actually supposed to read that paper. It has inappropriate content."

"You mean all those ads for escorts and massage therapists?" said Lynn.

"Well, not just that."

"She means that sex advice column," said Kas. "Not that I've ever read it. It's gross."

"Me, neither," said Lynn.

There was a pause.

Celia jumped in. "How do you know it's gross if you've never — "

Lynn and Kas started to laugh so hard that Mr. Aquasize glanced over.

Celia shook her head. "Oh, you guys."

"All right," said Kas, "as my colleague Celia would say, we have strayed from the point." She flipped through the pages. "Here it is. I Saw You. Okay. Here's one. 'Man to Woman. #9 bus. You: bright blue jacket, red hair. Me: green toque, beard. I gave my seat to a senior. You smiled at me. I wanted to talk. You, too?' Aw, doesn't Green Toque sound nice?"

"This is the perfect tool," said Celia. "And, look, it's online, too."

"Let's see," said Lynn. She ran her eye down the list. "But it's all, like, dating stuff."

"Who cares?" said Celia. "It might just work. Obviously lots of people read this paper, or at least, ahem ahem, *parts* of it. What details should we include?"

The exercise music stopped and the nifty sixties emerged from the pool, teasing and laughing, tossing their noodles and belts into the bin, flicking their heads to get water from their ears. The blue water calmed to glass and invited the girls in.

Kas stood up. "How about, 'You: green kilt. Me: chok-ing to death. You saved my life. Can we meet?'"

"It'll take some polishing," said Celia, "but the basic idea is great. Kilt identification and an I Saw You notice. A two-pronged approach." She stood up, licked the inside of her goggles, adjusting them over her eyes and did a tidy dive into the fast lane. Kas followed with more of a splash.

Lynn sat on the edge and watched the churning water. She was never one for diving in.

≈ ≈ ≈

THE GUINEA PIGS were loose on Celia's kitchen floor, cau-tiously inspecting Lynn's feet, rumbling and squeaking in their mysterious guinea-pig way. Celia, looking like a sur-geon in her rubber gloves and armed with a bottle of spray disinfectant, was cleaning out their cage. Kas was taking artsy guinea-pig photos and posting them to her blog.

"Come on, Hoover. Come on, Oreck, Miele. Smile for the camera."

"Okay," said Celia. "It's been a week. What progress have we made in our investigation of the identity of Heimlich girl?"

Kas consulted her phone. "Where are those tartans? Here we go. The three closest private schools use Arbuth-not Ancient, Modern Douglas and Hunting Gordon." She held out the screen to Lynn. "What do you think?"

"I don't know. Could be any of them."

"Inconclusive," said Celia. She scooped out some pine shavings. "What about the I Saw You ad?"

"A bust," said Lynn.

"No replies?"

"There were lots of replies, but all of them were from creeps. Looks like 'kilt' is some kind of code word."

"For what?" said Celia.

"Don't ask. Inappropriate content. Slimeball stuff."

"But they don't have your email address, right?" Celia was always careful about Internet safety.

"Right."

Kas shook her head. "I think we've hit the wall on the search."

"Yeah." Lynn slipped out of her sandals and wiggled her toes to give the guinea pigs a thrill. Some of the kilt replies had been seriously weird. Scary, even. Maybe it was time to let this go. "Do you think the Vacuums ever want to just make a break for freedom? Is Hoover saying, 'Come on, guys, this is our chance!'?"

Celia folded newspaper into precise squares. "Why would they? It's guinea-pig paradise right here. Best-quality hay, fresh veggies, vitamin C supplements, cuddle cups, plastic igloo, excellent conversation."

"I don't know," said Kas. "Sometimes cuddle cups aren't enough. Even if things are pretty good, sometimes you just want to escape. Like, I can hardly wait for Sunday, to just get on that choir bus and go."

"Me, too. Two sleeps and we're out of here." Lynn picked up Oreck.

"I'm kind of starting to get nervous," said Celia.

"Nervous?" said Lynn. "About performing?"

"No. Oh, I don't know. You'll think I'm stupid."

"Come on," said Kas. "When have you ever been stupid in your whole life?"

"Yeah," said Lynn. "Your bottom end of stupid is still above our top end of smart."

Celia exploded and laughed backwards up her nose. "My bottom end of stupid?"

Oreck, who liked a quiet life, gave a high-pitched squeak of distress.

"And, hey," said Kas. "Speak for yourself. I'm sure that my top end of smart at least touches Celia's bottom end of stupid. Once in a while. Well, once. Maybe in preschool. I was very smart in preschool. But, anyway, what are you nervous about?"

"The thing is … it's embarrassing."

"Oh, come on," said Lynn. "The Vacuums won't tell anybody."

"It's those shared bathrooms. At the college dorm where we're staying. I don't even like the bathrooms at school and there are going to be all those girls we don't even know and those rows of toilets. I bet they're the kind with gaps. In my family we're pretty private."

"Okay," said Kas. "Here's a promise. We'll find you a single toilet with a door. There's always one somewhere. A handicapped or something. You just have to look around and be a bit sneaky."

"But is that fair? What about if other people —"

"Stop! Stop with the fair thing. You have special needs. End. Of. Story."

Celia smiled. "Thanks, you guys. You're the best. Hey! Where did Miele get to? Miele? Miele?"

"Next topic," said Lynn. "What shoes are you taking?"

"Flats and low boots," said Kas. "Maybe runners."

"That reminds me," said Celia from the floor where she was crawling around, brandishing a stick of celery. "That instruction sheet said we should pack light so, since we're all going to be in the same room, should we share one hairdryer? I've got a travel one."

"Good idea," said Kas. "We need to leave room in our duffels because Mr. Inkpen said the bus could stop at the outlet mall on the way back. I'm going to buy stuff. I figure as long as I have my music, my choir clothes and my passport I'll be okay."

Passport. Lynn froze halfway to petting Hoover. What had happened about her passport? She filled out the application weeks ago, before things fell apart. She had her picture taken. She asked Shakti's friends Jean and Rob to be her guarantors. Shakti took the completed application for mailing. Lynn remembered seeing her stick stamps on it and stuff it into the chaos that was her bag.

Had it arrived? She hadn't seen it. Had Shakti just put it away without telling her?

She set Oreck in his cage, took out her phone and punched in Home.

No answer. Shakti's cell. *"The cellular party that you are trying to reach ... "*

Shoot. She laid Oreck gently in his cage.

"Sorry. Gotta go."

"Aren't you going to stay for stir-fry? Dad's cooking."

"No, something might be wrong. I'll text you."

FOUR

Return of the Glurb

As she rounded the corner to home, Lynn saw a man coming out the front door of her house. Her heart read "Clive" before her brain, the more sensible organ, realized it was a stranger. Nothing like Clive, really. Just male and dark-haired.

Was it one of those guys who was dealing with the soaking drywall?

No. Of course not. It must be Brandon. Of course. She hadn't planned to come home for dinner. Shakti wasn't expecting her.

He was wearing drop crotch pants. Oh, come on. How pathetic was that?

Which car was he heading toward? Not the Prius. That was Aileen-from-next-door's. Not Jag number two. That was Mr. Downley's organ donation vehicle for Jag number one.

Oh, no. He was coming right toward her. Didn't this loser even have a car?

Lynn panicked. Would he recognize her? Maybe — oh, gack — Shakti had even shown him a picture.

Lynn felt as though she was in a tunnel with no escape route.

She turned right abruptly, to the path heading toward the apartment building midway down the block. She went up to the intercom, walking slowly. She stared at the directory. Occupied, occupied, occupied, Satrous, occupied. The door clicked open and an old man came out pushing a walker. She held the door for him.

"Now, I can't let you come in," he said. "It seems so inhospitable but my daughter tells me that I'm not to let anybody into the building. She's a very suspicious person, my daughter. She always has been. She was a suspicious child. So I have to close the door and then you have to use the phone right there. Who was it that you wanted?"

"Um, I'm just going to visit my friend."

"Well, you have a nice visit. I'm going to get a paper. The crossword is very good on Friday."

Lynn slid a glance sideways. No Brandon. She stood trying to look like somebody impatiently waiting for a buzz-in. She slid a glance in the other direction. No Brandon.

She gave a sharp sigh and turned away from the door. The sidewalk was empty except for the man and his walker picking their way toward the newspaper box.

When she got in her front door she was met by the

now-familiar smell of wet drywall. Some guys had come and cut out a big piece of the basement wall, and now there were fans down there. Most of the contents of the basement had been moved upstairs, adding another layer of chaos to the existing post-Clive mess.

Lynn heard the sound of the kettle whistling in the kitchen. She walked through. Shakti was pouring water over coffee grounds.

"Hi."

"Ah!" Shakti started and spilled some water. "Oh. Lynn. Didn't expect you home for dinner."

Lynn saw her deciding whether to mention Brandon. She saw the yes.

"Did you encounter Brandon on the way in?"

Well, it wasn't exactly an encounter.

"No."

"I know. You're not ready yet. You have a good sense of your own limits."

Oh, gack. "Shakti. Where's my passport?"

"Your passport? You don't have a … oh." Shakti set down the coffee pot with precise care.

"My passport. You know. I gave you the application to mail about a month ago. It should have been here by now. I need it for Monday morning. You know. Portland."

"Oh, no. Did I mail that application? I remember you gave it to me. It was just before Clive left, right?"

"Yes."

"Wait." Shakti left the kitchen and came back with her

bag. She dumped it out onto the kitchen counter, knocking over the jar of coffee beans as she did so.

Lynn spied it right away — the gray envelope, fat and official.

"You forgot to send it in."

"Oh, I must have. It was such a confusing time. Oh, I'm so sorry. Are you absolutely sure you need a passport just to go on a school trip?"

Lynn didn't even bother to answer that stupidity. "You know this means I can't go."

"Oh, surely not. Come on. We'll look up the website and see what the rules are. Surely people have to get last-minute passports in a hurry. I'm sure we can find a way around this."

Click, click, click. There was no way around it. Even paying lots of money you could not apply for a passport at dinner time on Friday and get it by Sunday.

"This is unacceptable. What are people supposed to do if they have an emergency? It's because it's federal. If the government didn't spend so much money propping up their corporate cronies they could fund the passport service properly."

Lynn grabbed the mouse away from Shakti. "Stop clicking links! You've messed up! Admit it."

"Oh, Sixer, I'm so sorry. You must be feeling so disappointed. You were really looking forward to this trip, I know."

"Stop telling me what I must be feeling. You don't know

a thing about what I'm feeling. All you think about is you. You and Brandon." Lynn felt a sob creeping up her throat. She would not let herself cry.

"Ah, is this really about Brandon?"

"No. This is *not* about Brandon. This is about my passport. The passport I don't have."

Shakti angled her head the way she did when she was being understanding. All Lynn wanted to do was wipe that look off her face. From somewhere she got all the words, neatly packaged.

"You want to know what I was looking forward to the very most about the trip? The choir competition? Traveling on the bus with Kas and Celia and everybody? Singing? Outlet shopping? Missing school? No! It was escaping from you. You're useless. So useless that people are sorry for you. You don't even notice that, the way they look at you. Wherever you are, whatever you do, you just make things worse. No wonder Clive left. I just wish I could."

Something flashed across Shakti's face. Something fell away. Lynn hadn't meant to say that. Was it even true?

A small breeze made its way through the Venetian blinds. The slats fluttered and scraped against the window frame.

Shakti stood up, turned her back and began to scoop the coffee beans off the edge of the counter into her hand and then back into the jar, a few at a time.

Lynn walked to the door. "I have to phone Mr. Inkpen."

"Yes. Of course." Shakti turned. She swallowed. "Would you like me to do it and explain?"

"No."

Lynn got to her room, shoved music into her ears and lay down on her bed. According to Shakti, expressing anger was cleansing. So why did she feel like throwing up?

She pulled out her phone. There was a text from Kas.

Zup?

Her finger hovered over the Reply key. Until she answered, until she phoned Mr. Inkpen, it didn't have to be real.

≈ ≈ ≈

ON MONDAY, everybody at school was kind. The counselor, Ms. Yandle, had Lynn into the office to say how sorry she was to hear about the mix-up. The teachers were giving a pass on homework. Some girl she barely knew plunked down beside her at lunch saying, "Bummer about the choir thing," and offering a bag of chips. Between every class there were texts from Celia and Kas with details of Mr. Inkpen's bedhead, all the extra luggage Alexis had brought and how they started to sing in the customs hall at the border but the officials made them stop and how much they missed her, LYL.

But the day seemed long and pointless. It was a relief to be burped out into the rainy afternoon when the final buzzer rang.

There was the bus pulling into the stop. If the light turned green she could just make it.

She dodged the flagpole, cut across the grass and sprinted toward the street. The light stayed stubbornly red against her. She bounced on her toes and used her psychic powers. Turn! The bus loaded up and lumbered out into the traffic again just in time for the light to wink a sarcastic green.

Silver lining. There was plenty of room on the bus bench. Lynn inspected the backs of her legs. They were pock-marked with mud from her off-road run. Rain was making its way down her neck. She pulled up her hood.

Somebody slid onto the bench beside her. There was a whiff of fresh-turned soil.

"Would you like to be my friend?"

Lynn turned. Kilt, private-school coat, knee socks, pack. Brown hair pulled back.

It was her! She was holding a red umbrella that tinted her face pink.

"You! Wow. You're the one who gave me the Heimlich, right? So did you see our thing in I Saw You?"

The girl frowned. "I don't know what that is."

"Oh, okay. It's just this part in the free paper. For finding people. Mostly it's some guy who saw some hot girl on the bus and he was going to speak to her but then it looked like she was with some other guy and was she really and if not he was the one with the, like, pencil mustache."

"Mustache?" The girl was looking at her as though she was speaking algebra or something.

"Never mind. You're here! So. What's your name?"

"Blossom."

"Cool."

The girl smiled. "Is it? Is it a cool name?"

"Sure. Could be a singer or something. I'm Lynn. I know. Blah. It's not really a cool name but it's way better than my real name which, believe it or not, is Lindisfarne, which is this holy island over near England. My mom was into all that Celtic medieval stuff when I was born."

Lynn shook the drops off the edge of her hood. Why was she talking so much? She didn't usually spill the beans about her weird name right away.

"I've been looking for you. My friends were helping but we couldn't figure out what school you went to. I wanted to thank you. You saved my life. So ... um. Thank you."

"You're welcome. You wouldn't have found me. I was being invisible. I hear your bus approaching. Are you busy right now or can we visit?"

Approaching? Was this Blossom ESL or just formal? And did she just say that she could be invisible? Oh, boy. Either this extremely ordinary-looking person in a school uniform was a nutbar, or the world had become like one of those fantasy trilogies that Shakti liked to read and which were Lynn's least favorite books. Maybe this person was a glurb and she had an amulet that had to be restored to the true Druid princess or some such, and wouldn't it just be Lynn's luck if it turned out by some horrible cosmic joke that the world was really like that. She would have to go and lie down in the tundra somewhere and just give up.

The bus was poised at the light. On the other hand,

what was waiting at home? Shakti mess of all sorts. Maybe a glurb was just what she needed.

"Okay. What shall we do?"

FIVE

A Cup Full of Rain

BLOSSOM TOOK a very active approach to hanging out. She had a plan all ready to go.

"There's a guitarist at the rowboat dock at the lake. It's free. We could walk there in an hour."

An hour. That was quite a hike.

The rain was not a factor. Blossom reached into her pack and pulled out a polka-dot tube.

"Would you like an umbrella? This one has several features."

Who went around with two umbrellas? "Sure."

One of the features was a push button. The umbrella snapped into shape.

They set off, Blossom taking the lead. The route involved back alleys and cut-throughs. After about three turns, Lynn was completely turned around. What were the mountains doing *there*?

"We tried to trace you through your skirt. What school do you go to?"

"I don't go to school."

"Oh. Home schooled?"

"No. I don't go to school at all."

"So, what's with the uniform?"

"It's a citizen disguise. No. Sorry. I can't discuss that yet. Do you have any interests?"

Interests. Lynn felt like she was filling out a form. "Sure. Let's see. Mummification."

"Is that a common interest?"

"No. It's a joke."

Blossom nodded. "I thought it might be but you don't want to laugh at somebody's real interest."

She took an abrupt deke between two houses, calling over her shoulder, "What about clubs?"

This was a very weird conversation.

"Blossom, are you from somewhere else?"

"No. Here. What about clubs?"

Lynn felt a giggle starting to bubble up.

"Well, I'm in the school choir. That's for real. And, yes, that's a pretty common club. You?"

"No, I haven't had a chance to be in a club or youth group. What about hobbies?"

Hobbies! The bubble made its way rapidly northward from Lynn's stomach.

"Stop it! Stop it with the hobbies!" And then the word hobbies started to seem like some ridiculous, naughty pre-

school word like peanutbutterbum, and the next minute
Lynn was doubled over, snorting. She collapsed against the
fender of a car.

"Is saying hobbies like making a joke?" Blossom was
studying her intently. Her green eyes looked backlit.

"Not exactly. Hang on a minute." Lynn was madly min-
ing her pockets for a tissue to mop up her laughter-running
nose but all she came up with was pocket fluff, a bus transfer and one prehistoric and petrified Kleenex.

Blossom pushed something into her hand. It was white
and absorbent and it smelled like blueberry candles.

Lynn took off her glasses, mopped her eyes and nose
and then examined the white thing.

"Is this a sock?"

"Yes. They were a good find. A big box of them out
behind Behemoth's. All new. Too narrow for socks but excellent for other uses."

Behemoth's. "So that's why it smells like blueberry candles. Have you ever noticed that? All dollar stores smell like
blueberry candles." She stuck the sock into her pocket.

Blossom nodded. "It's not the same smell as blueberries." She ducked into a narrow lane between two stores.
"Come this way. It's a good cut-through."

"I'm laughing because you sound like some interviewer,
with your questions about interests and hobbies."

"Too many questions?"

"Kind of."

"I'm new to making friends. I read something in a library magazine. A magazine for teenagers. It said you should ask about the other person's interests. And then suggest a mutual activity."

Going to the library to look up how to make friends, and then admitting it. There was something about this girl, something so uncool that it almost met the distant back end of extremely cool.

Blossom's style of walking favored back alleys and hidden features. The backwards house, the bubble-blowing equipment nailed to a telephone pole, the little free library, the graveyard of faded pink plastic flamingos, the raccoon family living in a derelict hot tub, the abandoned car with a tree growing up through the middle, the tin can fountain, the backyard skateboard ramp, the raven's nest.

"Have you ever seen those shrubs cut into the shape of chess pieces? It's worth a detour."

Lynn felt like a tourist in an unknown city.

After about an hour they came around the corner of a community center to the edge of a small lake and the sounds of a guitar.

The guitarist was sitting cross-legged on the dock under a rigged-up tarp. A bouquet of umbrellas nestled around him. He had a copper-colored shaved head and square-tipped fingers. He looked varnished, like his guitar. Hunched over, he seemed to have grown around his instrument. His face was a calm mask except for a little twitch near his left eye.

"Is he busking?" Lynn whispered. "His guitar case isn't open."

"Sometimes he does. Maybe not today."

A fine mist rose from the lake and inside it the music was fast, faster, fastest, disappearing fingers, each note washed by raindrops, a scrape up the neck and then those high ping sounds that seemed to get into your body by some route other than your ears. Behind it all was the drum section of rain on the tarp and on umbrellas.

Someone in the audience called out a word. Lynn couldn't make out what it was. The guitarist gave a half-nod and slid the melody into something absolutely simple. One note at a time, walking pace, repeating like the warm-ups at choir. Then he reached up and retuned the strings while he was playing, and the whole thing changed color.

Then it was done. People tried to clap and their umbrellas went sideways and everybody laughed. The musician laid his guitar in the case and turned ordinary — awkward, not great teeth, one of those nerdy jackets with too many pockets. The listeners gave each other pleased smiles and little nods and then slid away into the rain.

The dry zone under the tarp, still inhabited by wisps of music, invited the girls to settle.

"Was this a fun mutual activity?" Blossom asked, her gaze level and calm.

"Yes. Yes, it was."

"The magazine said that friends talk about plans and feelings."

Maybe it was the moment of the day, when things disengage before changing gear. Maybe it was the place or maybe it was just this girl. She made Lynn want to crack up and cry at the same time.

It tumbled out. Shakti and the claw-handed chandelier and Clive and the flood and Choirfest and married Brandon. All the mess of the past few weeks.

Somebody turned up the volume of the rain. The tarp began to sag. Lynn pulled her feet farther into the dry zone.

Blossom didn't comment. She just listened but her listening was so intense that Lynn found herself saying something she had never said aloud. She looked out through the mist walls of the floating room.

"Sometimes I hate her."

"Yes."

Lynn turned to meet Blossom's eyes, the quiet gaze of a sudoku master, concentrating as though Lynn were a stray eight that needed a box and a column and a row to be in.

Blossom frowned slightly. "I have a question."

Lynn was too busy swallowing to speak. She was going to need another sock, any second. She nodded.

"Is this a typical citizen family?"

"Um, I don't really get the question. What's the citizen thing?"

"Citizens. That's you."

"And not you?"

"No."

"Are you a new immigrant or illegal or something?"

"No." Blossom bit her bottom lip. "I'm an Underlander. Oh. I'm not allowed to tell you about us. That's a rule.

We have to be invisible to citizens. But I wanted to find a friend. Tron used to be my friend but now he acts like he's ashamed of us. And I love Larch but he's fearful of so much. And I've been reading stories from the library about citizen girls and their friends. They all have friends. And then I saved your life so I thought I would try to be your friend because if you were already my friend I would know that I could trust you and then I could tell Fossick about you, but I have so many questions and I can't really answer any of your questions because I am already disobeying him and all the books say that friendship is supposed to be equal."

In the middle of this confusing declaration, Blossom's voice started to wobble. Any minute now she was going to need a sock, too. Lynn leaned over and grabbed her hand.

"Hey. It's okay. You don't need to tell me one single thing. You can just be mystery woman."

"Really?"

"Really. We can even have a code word. If I ask you about something that you're not allowed to talk about, you can just say, like, pretzel or something. Try it. Come on. Who the heck is Fossick?"

"Um. Pretzel?"

"You got it."

Blossom grinned, reached into her pack and took out a plastic cup. "Thirsty?"

Lynn nodded. "But I've got my own water bottle."

"Wait, this is better." Blossom held the cup out beyond the tarp and then took her umbrella and pushed up the baggy tarp roof. A great whoosh of water drained off, filling the cup to the brim. Blossom plucked out a single leaf and offered the water to Lynn.

Drinking the rain. How odd. How perfectly ordinary. How delicious.

"Okay. I didn't answer your question. No, we're not a typical citizen family. Shakti is not typical of anything. My friends Kas and Celia, their families are more typical, I guess. Two parents married to each other, that's the usual citizen thing."

Lynn handed the half cup of rain back to Blossom.

"These friends. Do you tell them everything?"

"Not exactly everything."

Blossom set down the cup and beamed her sudoku gaze.

"You can't tell them or anyone else about me. You have to keep me a secret. It's important. If the authorities find out about us we could lose everything. Our home. Each other. You must make a solemn vow."

Solemn vow? The authorities? Even if there were no amulets, this person in a kilt was definitely from another world. What had she said? An Underlander? Was this a cult or something? But Blossom just didn't have the border-line crazy look of those ones with the pamphlets. She just seemed, well, some combination of young and old and, more than anything, real.

Feeling half like a kid doing a pinkie swear and half like a witness taking an oath in court, Lynn replied, "Okay. I promise. I mean, I make a solemn vow."

Blossom exhaled. "Thank you. Thank you, Lindisfarne. That's a joke. Well, more a tease than a joke. Next time we can talk about hobbies. That's another joke. Now I'll go."

It could have been abrupt but it was just clear and tidy. And there was to be a next time?

"Um, Blossom?"

"Yes."

"I don't actually know how to get back."

"Oh." Blossom looked around and thought for a second or two. "The nearest stop for your bus is four blocks south and one block east."

"And that's …"

"Oh, sorry." She pointed. "That direction. Then turn left."

"Cool. Great. Here's your umbrella."

Blossom shook her head. "No, it's for you. Umbrellas are an easy find." Then she headed off into the trees at the edge of the lake and was gone. Invisible girl.

Lynn whapped the umbrella open. Polka dots. Secretly she still loved polka dots. Were there once some polka-dot overalls?

She twirled the umbrella before heading out into the wet and noticed something odd. All collapsible umbrellas died the same death. The ends of the spokes became detached from the fabric, leaving flapping nylon and naked metal points that threatened to put out the eyes of fellow pedestrians. When that happened, the umbrellas ended up in a garbage bin, like so many dead herons.

But this umbrella featured ingenious little reinforcements at the end of each spoke. Neatly sewn in rainbow colors, they were obviously a post-production addition, and done by hand.

Who would take the time to mend an umbrella?

SIX

Cottage Country

CHOIR BLOCK, last block of the day. No choir. No choir teacher. Everyone was still being kind, and the vice-principal had suggested she just go home early. Once that would have been a treat. Back in ancient times, a month ago. Back when home was normal.

Now, not so much.

"I think I'll go to the resource center and catch up on some homework."

The veep looked impressed.

The resource center was quiet and deserted. Lynn settled into one of the armchairs and took out her phone. She was on Clive's cellphone plan. How much longer would he keep paying for that? She didn't even know how much it cost. She was going to have to know how much things cost. She took that worry and shelved it.

There were texts, lots of texts, from Kas and Celia. They

were being excellent friends, reporting regularly. The big news, overwhelming even the choir competition itself, was that big-hair, big-voice Alexis was discovered drunk in the room of some boy from McMinville and she was being sent home but first they had to wait for her mother to come and get her.

Would Celia be singing the solo? What was going to happen to Alexis? What was going to happen to the boy? Where the heck was McMinville? Lynn sent back appropriate replies full of punctuation, but even as she typed she found her mind wandering.

Actually, her mind had wandered for days, and always the wander ended with a girl in a kilt drinking rain. She had gone over every bit of their odd conversation.

Blossom. She idly typed it into the phone. An old TV series. What kind of series? When? She waited for a message from a cloud. Oh, this was way too slow. She pushed herself out of the armchair and sat down at a computer.

Blossom. A science definition, a singer named Blossom Dearie, something about start-ups. Peaseblossom, a fairy in Shakespeare. Fairies, hmm. Click, click, click. *A species completely independent of humans or angels.* She seemed independent, all right. *Noted for mischief and malice toward humankind.* Not noted for saving their lives, apparently.

On the basis of the evidence she was probably not a fairy.

The real question, and there was no link for that, was when and where was Blossom going to turn up again? What and where and if? Bus stop? Well, it would have to be. Unless she was going to be down by the lake. Should Lynn go there and have a look? Today? No, probably today was too soon. When Blossom said, "Next time," she probably meant next week, or even a few weeks.

The buzzer ripped through Lynn's thoughts, and she went to her locker to pack up, to send a few more exclamation marks to the Diode and to delay what she was sure was going to be a disappointment at the bus stop.

Blossom wasn't at the bus stop. She was right outside the front door of the school, bouncing on the balls of her feet and smiling with her whole face. Students flowed around her like she was some rock in a river.

She handed Lynn an envelope. "He said you could visit. Open it."

The envelope had a window, like a bill, and it was covered with intricate doodles. Through the plastic window Lynn could see the message: YOU'RE INVITED.

It was too pretty to rip, so Lynn eased open the flap. The card inside was a match of lacy doodles.

> What: A Visit with Blossom and Larch
> Where: The Cottage
> When: Today

"This is beautiful."

"Larch made it. He spent all morning. He's very excited. Me, too. Last night I talked to Fossick for a long time. I told him all about the bus stop and the concert and you and wanting a friend. He was worried because of you being a citizen but I told him you were trustworthy and he said he thought I had good judgment and of course things had to change as I got older because nothing gold can stay. He said I could invite you for a visit, but we shouldn't overwhelm you so it is just me and Larch. For a friendly visit. Can you come?"

A chance to untwist some of the pretzels? Of course she would go.

From the moment that they ducked into a driveway beside the dry cleaner, it was another zigzag route, as though there was a shadow grid underneath the official grid of the city.

Lynn picked questions at random.

"Where's this cottage?"

"In the Lingerlands. You'll see." Blossom stopped so abruptly that Lynn ran into the back of her. "This is an important part of the friendly visit. You can never tell anyone the location of the cottage."

"Got it. Solemn vow." Lingerlands. This was moving quickly back into glurb territory.

"What's with the uniform?"

"It's a citizen disguise."

"Why not just wear pants and a hoodie or something?"

"I used to. That's what the boys wear. But Tron found this. All the parts — shirt, jacket, skirt, raincoat, even shoes. The whole thing was a throwaway and it's so beautiful. It all goes together properly so that I can be invisible."

"But why do you need to be in disguise?"

"It's important that we're not noticed."

"Why?"

"We're not official."

Official? What did that mean? "Who's we?"

"Our family. We're Fossick, my father, and Tron and Larch, my brothers."

Each answer opened out into more questions, like a flow chart.

"What's the deal about citizens? Are you, like, immigrants from some other country or something?"

The explanation that followed was as zigzag as the path they were following. But as Blossom described living "off the grid" and a complicated life of "finds" and the rules and work and the garden, the truth hit Lynn.

A secret location, gardening, making a living without a job?

Of course. It was a marijuana grow-op.

Maybe this wasn't such a good idea. This family with the weird names? They might be bad news. And weren't those places full of toxic chemicals and, like, guns? What was that news story? Some grow-op in the interior had been guarding their marijuana fields with a grizzly bear.

"... Fossick says we come from under the ground like the strong grass and the lovely trees. Here we are. The Lingerlands."

It wasn't a glurb world after all, but the familiar reservoir park. People in bright clothes played pitch and putt. A Chinese senior walked backwards up a gentle hill. There were some warning signs about coyotes but no mention of grizzlies.

This would be the place to bail. This was so not making a good choice.

But it was only going to be a visit. Like a field trip. And besides, Blossom seemed the opposite of dangerous.

"How much farther?"

"We're close now. We came the long way round for security. We change our path often."

They walked along the running path for a few minutes and then Blossom, with a glance forward and back, slipped into the tangle of untended shrubs and ground cover that ringed the path. Lynn followed, sharp twigs grabbing for her hair, and vines tangling themselves around her feet. Down a gentle dip there was another path, narrow and rough like the path of animals, another concrete wall, another ring of the reservoir. Along that wall were things you would never notice because they were boring — metal screens, pipes, ducts, squares of metal.

Blossom paused at one of the screens, pulled a key from her pocket and pulled it across the metal net, creating an eerie, shimmering sound.

"That lets Larch know we're here," she said.

A few steps later, she pushed aside some hanging vines, revealing a square the size and shape of a door. She slid aside a thin metal strip at the top left of the door to reveal a keypad. She punched some keys and there was a soft but official click, and the door edged open.

"This is it?"

Blossom nodded. "Don't tarry. We like to get in and out neatly."

Lynn hesitated. Tarry? Who said tarry? Blossom grabbed her by the arm and pulled her over the threshold. "Come *on*."

The door clicked definitively shut behind them.

Inside there was no dragon lair, no tapping of elvish miners, no stalagmite-encrusted cave. Lynn's first impression was that it was like being inside a machine. It was warm and there was a low hum. Small lights glinted on the ceiling. Pipes snaked overhead. It was all hard-edged, metal, businesslike. It was very clean. It smelled like nothing.

Blossom led the way through a labyrinth of pillars and pipes.

"Watch your head."

Then they came to a blank white wall. As Blossom pressed on it and it began to slide open, the story in Lynn's head changed again. How Nancy Drew was this?

As the wall opened, it was like the curtain parting on a set that was a combination of trailer, tent, kid's hidey-hole under the dining-room table, animal den, garage sale and attic junk room.

Everything was layered. Rug on rug. The walls were a collage of pictures, maps, charts and small shelves covered in little creatures made of nuts and bolts. There were five or six chairs that seemed to be made of slotted-together cardboard, piled with cushions. The walls were a patchwork of doors.

There were strings of Christmas lights looped around. A shaft of sunlight reflecting off a mirror set into a big pipe in the ceiling made a spotlight on the floor. A table, three doors long, was covered with tools and tin cans full of bits of things, and a big pile of empty toilet-paper rolls. Stalagmites of books grew up from the floor. Wire baskets hanging from the ceiling held fruits and vegetables, packets and packages. In one corner five bicycles were neatly parked.

"Where are the plants?" said Lynn.

"What plants?"

Recalculating! Nothing to do with a grow-op. "Um, house plants?"

"Oh. There isn't really enough light for plants inside. We have a garden, though. Some day we'll take you there. Do you have plants at your house?"

Lynn did not get a chance to explain the skeleton fig tree in their living room, because one of the doors — the doors that seemed like a wall — opened. A boy and a dog stepped into the hodgepodge room. The dog looked like a map of an island world, white with precise black patches. He stood knee-high next to the boy and seemed to be smiling.

The boy had long, fine, curly, glass-colored hair and a pale face with a high forehead. There was something familiar about the face but Lynn couldn't place it. He was hard to read.

How old was he? Younger than her or older? He was taller, but plump like some of those short boys at school who hadn't stretched out yet. There was something about the way he stood that wasn't like a boy, yet not like a girl, either. He hunched his shoulders and stared at the floor like a shy kindergartener, but he was dressed like a man, in a suit, a rumpled shirt and a bright tie with slashes of color.

Blossom put her hand on his shoulder. "Larch, this is my friend Lynn."

The boy nodded. "The visitor. Welcome. When we have a visitor we tidy up before she comes, we welcome her, we introduce Artdog, this is Artdog, who is named Artdog because he looks like a piece of op art, short for optical art, which is a style of art mostly in black and white, we offer her something to eat and then we talk."

Artdog whapped his tail on the floor and Larch reached behind one of the many curtains and brought out a plate. He handed it to Lynn.

Neatly arranged were a package of raisins, a carrot, a piece of lettuce, a chocolate cream puff and a small lime yogurt.

"There is construction on the Mary Hill Bypass. What does the visitor think about that?"

All the time he looked away, into the distance or down to the floor.

Lynn bit into the carrot and glanced at Blossom, who gave her a small nod.

"Thank you, Larch. Um, about the Mary Hill Bypass. I don't know too much about it. What are they constructing?"

Larch stood considering. "The traffic report didn't say. The traffic report said that traffic is congested back to the Delta Works Yard and drivers are advised to use Highway 10 instead. What do you think? Is this a good conversation for a visitor?"

Lynn was stopped in her tracks before she realized that the question was directed at Blossom.

"Yes, it's up-to-date and you asked the visitor's opinion. Well done." She turned to Lynn. "We don't have many visitors, so Larch and I practiced. How are we doing?"

At this point Larch turned his face to Lynn, not quite meeting her gaze. His eyes were blueberry blue. His face was scrubbed — not just clean but scrubbed of cool, scrubbed of any mask. He looked like an angel on a Christmas card. Not a cute angel but an art angel.

"You're doing great. I feel very welcomed. Here are two more things about visitors. Usually everybody sits down and shares the food."

"Oh, good," said Larch, reaching over to grab the cream puff and launching himself into a chair. Artdog jumped into his lap. The cardboard must have been stronger than it looked. He licked his fingers and declared, to some corner of the room, "Larch loves cream puffs."

Blossom held up one finger. "Who loves cream puffs?"

Larch gave his head a shake. "I love cream puffs."

"Good," said Blossom. "Come on, Lynn, pick a chair."

Lynn fell into a sea of cushions and plucked one question from the mystery that settled around her.

"Where are we? What is this place? I mean, what was it before it was your house?"

"It's one of the forgotten places. Fossick says it was some kind of construction storage area when they were building the reservoir. It got walled off."

"How did you guys find it?"

"Fossick discovered it, before I was born. He likes to look around behind things. He says that even in a city there are many places unaccounted for. I've lived here my whole life."

"So what about your other brother? Tron, was it? How old is he?"

"He's seventeen."

Larch's face darkened. "He's seventeen and he's bad! He's not doing his work." He started to flap his hands.

Blossom leaned over and put both hands on the top of Larch's head, making a cap with her fingers. "We can talk about that later."

"What do you do about ... I mean, do you have a bathroom?"

Larch giggled. "Of course we do!"

"What's with all the doors?"

Blossom rattled some raisins into Lynn's hand.

"Doors are an easy find. Doors and beds and couches and books and ties. Citizens leave them in an alley or on the street. Also exercise bicycles. Why do citizens make bicycles that go nowhere? Tron takes them apart for good pieces. The other left-outs are always plastic toys and those magazines with yellow covers."

"They have pictures of every place in the world," said Larch. "Deep sea exploration, Shangri-La, crop circles in Switzerland. That's what Larch is working on now."

Lynn had a vision, a kind of old-fashioned cartoon, of two space aliens — green, big eyes, head boppers, from separate planets — meeting beside some asteroid and trying to explain their ways to each other. She was responsible for making sense of exercise bikes and the tons of National Geographics that must be out there somewhere. Blossom was responsible for explaining angel-boy and his "work" and "finds" and if they weren't growing marijuana down here how were they making a living but, more to the immediate point, where was that bathroom?

The bathroom had a shower, a sink, and an odd toilet that she had to climb up to. There was a complicated tangle of plastic pipes like a plate of noodles and some stiff, scratchy towels. There was a cat asleep on one of the larger pipes.

When she got back to the hodgepodge room, cat shadowing her, Larch had fallen asleep in his chair with Artdog curled up at his feet, smiling even as he slept.

"Catmodicum found you," said Blossom. "I should tell you. She doesn't know she's a cat."

Lynn spoke softly. "What's with Larch?"

"Oh, he naps all the time. It's his way. All the excitement of your visit has worn him out. Fossick said it might."

"Where is Fossick?"

"He's working. It's Returns day."

"Is he really okay with me being here? I know you're pretty private."

"My birthday's coming up. On our birthdays Fossick says we can have our heart's desire, if it's humanly possible. And my heart's desire was to have a friend my own age."

"You never wanted that before?"

Blossom frowned. "Tron was always my friend. He took me with him wherever he went. He taught me things. We had fun. But then something happened and now he doesn't even seem to like me. Or any of us. He doesn't come home. He's grumpy and disrespectful to Fossick. He isn't here to take care of Larch. All he wants to do is be with those homeless soccer guys and that's stupid because we're not homeless!" Blossom slapped her chair and then sank lower into it.

"But he's seventeen, right?"

"Yes."

"Then that's kind of normal. I mean, I'm no expert, but the older brothers of my friends? They don't hang out with us."

Blossom gave Lynn the sudoku stare. Her voice was small. "Do they stop loving their sisters?"

"Oh ..." Lynn was trying to figure out what to say to such a sad question, when Artdog gave a sharp yip and Larch sat up, apparently instantly awake.

"Would the visitor like to listen to music? We have every kind."

Lynn glanced at her phone. It was late.

"That would be great, Larch, but I need to get home. Thank you for your hospitality. I had a great time."

"Yes, you did. When the visit is over we thank the visitor and invite her to come again."

Blossom walked Lynn through the machine area to the door.

"Blossom? About Tron? Really, I don't think teenagers stop loving their families. It's just that they turn into jerks for a while."

"That's what happens with citizens?"

"Not just citizens. Humans. And maybe animals, too. Who knows? For all we know maybe teenage … tunafish are all rude and horrible."

"Tunafish?" Blossom grinned. "So. Larch says we invite the visitor to come again. Will you come to my birthday party on Saturday? To meet the others? We'll have wonderful food, all boughten."

Whatever boughten food was, Lynn was going to be there.

Heimlich girl and the citizen, two space aliens floating away from their planets and meeting, by the slimmest of chances, in outer space, green hands touching.

"Sure."

SEVEN

Youth Cred

"Lynn, I hope you can be here for dinner tomorrow. I'm going to do that three-cheese lasagna that you love. And company's coming."

Shakti sounded weirdly tentative, and Lynn thought she knew why. This was it. This was going to be the big Meet Brandon moment. There was no lasagna in the world that would lure her to such an event. She had her answer ready. She knew exactly how to deflect Shakti by talking the talk. The answer was going to be, This is a big change for me and I don't think I'm ready.

"So, who's the company?"

"Jean and Rob."

Oh. Recalculate.

Jean and Rob were friends of Shakti's from back when dinosaurs walked the earth. They had real jobs and they stuck with them. Rob was a longshoreman and Jean was

70

an accountant for non-profits. They were vegetarians and foster parents and community organizers. Best of all, they were quiet about it, quiet and funny. They made as little of themselves as Shakti made much of herself. Lynn once overheard that Jean was registered as an unrelated bone marrow donor, which meant you went in and had painful surgery and took risks for somebody that you didn't even know.

They had stood by Shakti through thick and thin. What did that expression mean, anyway? Were the thicks the good times and thin the bads?

Lynn's phone pinged a message. She pulled it out to check. It was Celia. *Mega news. Phone RIGHT NOW.*

"Lynn. Please don't read your phone while I'm talking to you. It makes me feel like a piece of furniture. Dinner tomorrow?"

"Oh. Yeah. Okay."

Lynn went up to her room and flopped on her bed. Kapok stared, obviously dying to know the news of the Diode.

Celia started out the report. Kas was in the speakerphone background.

"So, the guy from McMinville got sent back home last night and his whole choir hates our choir because they say that Alexis seduced him. They are calling Alexis horrible names."

"Skanky," piped up Kas.

"Anyway, the guy, whose name is Romeo, if you can believe it — "

"Get out."

"Pronounced Rome-AY-oh," corrected Kas.

"He says that his family is going to sue the school. But, anyway, Romeo — "

"Rome-*AY*-oh."

"Whatever, had the strongest male voice and now the McMinvilles think they don't have a chance and they're blaming us. And the second round concert is tonight."

Kas's voice boomed out. "And what Celia is way too modest to tell you is that she is doing the solo."

Lynn bounced off her bed. "Celia! That's amazing! Go girl! Kas, fist-bump her for me."

Clunk. "Oh, sorry. I fist-bumped the phone."

"I'm kind of nervous," said Celia. "You know, being the center of attention. Braces and all that."

"Those aren't braces," boomed Kas. "Those are bling! Oh, Lynn, everyone is so pumped. This morning I caught Travis actually practicing scales. We're going to slaughter McMinville."

"Hey, give me the phone back. Lynn, we're so sorry that you're not here. We miss you every single note. We're … bummed."

"Awww." Lynn felt a little catch in her throat. Bummed was strong language from Celia. "Celia, I have two words for you. Canadian Idol."

Celia giggled.

"Gotta go. One last practice. We are so breathing from the diaphragm. We've got diaphragms of steel."

"Okay. Be awesome. Hugs. Send pictures."

Lynn flopped back onto her pillows. She tried to imagine telling this story to Blossom. Citizen high school. It would involve a lot of explanations.

≈ ≈ ≈

FRIDAY LYNN stayed late at school working on a skit for French. By the time she got home, Jean and Rob had already arrived. They were sitting at the table under the claw, deep into glasses of wine and a conversation with Shakti, discussing an upcoming political protest. The smell of lasagna almost covered up the smell of wet drywall.

"Hi, gorgeous," said Rob, pulling another chair up to the table. "Take a pew."

"It's those scumbag developers," said Shakti. "That land was set aside for public housing but now council's going to let them build a casino on it."

"Wrong on so many fronts," said Rob.

"We just need to make our point. I'm sure they'll listen to creative dissent," said Jean, the world's most optimistic person.

"It's two weeks tomorrow," said Shakti. She reached over and touched Lynn's shoulder. "Would you like to join us, Sixer?"

Her voice was quiet and unsure. Ever since Lynn had unhooked, Shakti had become smaller, diminished. It should have been a relief, but instead it made her want to shake her mother. Don't be so *feeble*!

But what about the invitation? Lynn had grown up on protests — the baby in the stroller, the toddler with a message on her T-shirt, the middle-schooler singing along. The box of photos was full of shots of marches and banners. There were always other kids and usually candy and little bags of chips and Shakti being happy. No Clive, though. Clive always said, "I don't do chanting. How about I just write a check."

"We'd love for you to be there, hon," said Jean.

Jean and Rob … they were good to be with.

"Okay, but do we have to carry signs?"

Shakti lit up. "No! That's the brilliant part. It's going to be a different sort of protest. The developers are meeting at a downtown hotel, having some expensive bribing lunch for all the big influential people on council and the investors and the media — busloads of them, apparently. There's a plan for a flash event to disrupt it."

"We need to get the word out," said Rob.

"I can help with that," said Shakti. "I've got flexible time at the moment. Anybody for lasagna?"

"How's the job search coming?" asked Jean.

Lynn waited for the answer. As far as she could see, there had been no efforts in that direction.

"I know it's out there. I'm not going to push it and take some stopgap thing. I've made that mistake before."

"Well, anything we can do to help," said Rob. "Jean's got a jazzy new printer if you want to copy your resume."

Shakti nodded. "Hmmm."

"Back to immediate plans," said Jean. "We're supposed to dress corporate. I'm not sure I can manage."

"Of course you can," said Shakti. "If I can do corporate, you can do corporate. We just need to go to that snazz consignment store, X-Threads. They specialize in business casual." She glanced at her watch. "We can go tonight."

"All right, then," said Jean. "On two conditions. One is that Lynn comes, too, to lend her youth cred. The other is that you both come to our place for pie after." She grinned at Lynn. "Deal?"

Lynn wasn't so sure about her fashion cred, but it was never an option to pass on Jean's pies.

"Sure."

"Count me out," said Rob. "I'll wear my wedding and funeral suit. Clothes life is easier for men." He held up one hand to signal stop. "I know. I know. Life is *always* easier for men. Point conceded."

≈ ≈ ≈

JEAN STOOD at the door of X-Threads.

"I don't want to go in. I'm scared."

"Jean! You're the one who stared down armed bandits on that bicycle trip to Malaysia. How can you be afraid of a clothing store? A used clothing store?"

"I just am. They'll be scornful. I'm not their ilk."

"Nonsense." Shakti opened the door with a flourish and ushered Jean and Lynn inside.

It turned out that Jean was absolutely right about ilks.

She kept gravitating to fleece and Shakti to feathers. She was wrong, however, about the sales clerks, who although fashionable and skinny turned out to be totally supportive of the project, not to mention tactful.

"That's an interesting retro piece, but not corporate."

"It's retro?" said Jean.

"Good color but several sizes too large for you."

"But it's so *comfortable*."

"Yes, the colors are beautiful and tie-dyed silk can work in an ironic kind of way, but not in this context."

"Irony?"

Clothes piled up in the fitting rooms and the younger of the clerks finally gave Lynn a pleading look.

"Look," said Lynn. "Don't think clothes, think costume. Think Halloween."

Energized by the idea of being a corporate witch, Jean finally agreed to heels and a plain black skirt suit with a print shirt to "pop it up."

"Ruffles?" She had to sit down in a chair to recover. "Oh, Lynn, thank goodness you're with us. But what about your disguise?"

"I've got the perfect thing," said the older clerk, holding out a navy blue wool trench coat.

Lynn slipped it on. It was actually very cool.

"I think you've found your look," said Shakti. "Junior high corporate."

"I think it's more like espionage," said Jean. "It would go nicely with a foggy night and a cigarette in a cigarette holder. Oh, crikey, sorry. I know I'm not supposed to glamorize smoking." One of the cracks in Jean's armor of goodness was that she was a die-hard smoker.

"On that subject …" She looked outside longingly.

"Go," said Shakti.

The clerks then applied themselves to Shakti, glamming and accessorizing, dressing up and dressing down. Between outfits they became Amanda and Jasmin, Shakti's new best friends.

The final choice was a dark gray pencil skirt with a silver-gray jacket. The collar of the jacket stood up, framing her face.

"We've been just waiting for the perfect person for that jacket," said Amanda.

"Yes," said Jasmin. "That is going to take you anywhere you want to go."

Amanda gave an appraising look. "Can it handle pearls, do you think?"

"Absolutely," said Jasmin, draping a necklace over Shakti's head.

She looked … Lynn stepped outside herself for a moment and admitted it. She looked stunning.

"Okay," said Amanda. "Give us your best CEO look."

Shakti did a little pout thing with her mouth, tossed her head back and said, "By all means move at a glacial pace. You know how that thrills me."

Amanda exploded. "Miranda Priestly in *Devil Wears Prada*!" She and Shakti did a little squirmy happy dance.

Jasmin caught Lynn's eye, smiled, shrugged and shook her head.

≈ ≈ ≈

THERE WERE TWO kinds of pie — rhubarb-strawberry and something called sunburnt lemon. Lynn had both kinds.

Jean and Shakti tried on their outfits and Rob said they looked beautiful and scary.

"Should we shave our legs?" asked Jean.

Shakti propped one leg up on a footstool. "I think so. It's the least we can do if we really want to topple the corporate superstructure."

Jean snorted. "Remember that cabaret thing we were in back in the day, body hair the last frontier?"

Lynn stood up and gathered dishes. Some conversations you just didn't want to overhear.

She rinsed the plates, ate one more sliver of sunburnt lemon and looked around the kitchen, almost as familiar as her own. She looked at the collage of the corkboard. Meetings, fundraisers, petitions, political flyers, photos of foster kids who had passed through. Clutter, projects, memories, things happening and about to happen.

It was like the cottage.

The voices drifting in from the other room got louder.

"Shaving your legs is not the same as shaving off my beard. I refuse."

There was a chorus of friendly argument followed by

Rob bellowing, "Why, why, why, Delilah!" Next thing was the tinny sound of music.

"Lynn! Come back. Stop working. You're missing Tom Jones."

The three were crowded around the laptop where some grotesque guy was singing a song about stabbing his girl-friend, backed up with an oompah-pah band.

"They're coming to get him because he murdered her, right?" said Lynn.

"No," said Rob. "They're coming to arrest him because of his sideburns."

Shakti grabbed a rolled-up magazine and started to lip-sync.

"You're good at that," said Jean. "You completely get the look. Regret and guilt combined with the pain of acid reflux."

"I missed my calling," said Shakti.

Lynn wondered for a moment if it might be true. Shak-ti at her best, charming Amanda and Jasmin, wearing the corporate look as though she did it every day, being Tom Jones — that Shakti just disappeared in muddle and mess. Was there a calling she had somehow missed?

Lynn pulled herself together. What was she doing, try-ing to explain her mother? It was a waste of time, a waste of brain cells.

Jean put on her new shoes and teetered around the room.

"I'm going to have to go into training. I've got two weeks to master this skill."

"Who else is going to be there?" said Lynn.

"Oh, the usual suspects," said Rob. "We're hoping for some of those younger Battle in Seattle folks. You should bring some friends along."

"Maybe." It *would* be better to have some friends along. Celia was out of the question. Her parents thought civil disobedience was a criminal activity. Kas would probably be up for it, but Saturday mornings were soccer, and soccer was sacred.

But what about ... ? This was certainly a fun mutual activity, and Blossom was already in a kind of corporate disguise.

Would that be possible?

EIGHT
Finding Day

"STAY ON THE LINE for a big announcement." Kas made trumpet fanfare noises.

"Okay," said Lynn. "I'm ready and waiting."

"Hold it, why do you sound so muffled?"

"I'm volumizing. Remember you told me that I can plump up my hair by hanging it upside down for twenty minutes a day?"

"Yes, well, forget plump hair at this moment. Heeeeeeere's Celia!"

"We won!"

"What? You won the whole thing?"

"Yup. Best choir at the festival. Take that, McMinville!"

"O.M.G. That is awesome!"

"And … Celia! Give me the phone. Celia blew them away with her solo."

"Lynn? I really did. Something happened. Like, something happened to my body. This voice came out from nowhere, like the choir behind me was a wave and I was a surfer."

"Singing surfer dude! Well, dudette, I guess. Celia, that's amazing. Bet Inky's happy, eh?"

"He cried! Spilling-over-tears cried."

"Lynn, I'm so sorry that you weren't here. That was the only bad thing. What's up back there?"

"Well, you know. The usual. I caught a glimpse of Brandon."

Kas jumped back in. "Get out. What's he look like?"

"Dark hair. Kind of short. Drop crotch pants."

"Drop crotch! That's just sad."

"I'm getting free blocks where choir used to be. Sabrina Durmaz and I are doing a French skit together. I can tell you all the other stuff when you get home. Tomorrow, right?"

"No. That's the other big news. The winning choir gets to stay a whole week longer and do some concerts."

"Bummer. No, I mean, that's great but I miss you."

"Miss you, too."

"Miss you squared."

Lynn tucked her phone away. The usual. Hardly. She was about to leave for what might be the most unusual birthday party of her life. She didn't know what to expect, but she didn't think that a sushi party platter and a rented karaoke machine would be involved.

≈ ≈ ≈

A T'AI CHI GROUP with swords was going through their paces as Lynn reached the fountain, the designated meeting place. As the water rose and fell behind her, she sat on the concrete edge and watched the ballet.

She was looking forward to meeting mysterious Fossick and bad Tron but mostly she wanted to see Larch again. During that first visit when Blossom put her hands on his head to calm him, when she encouraged him to say "I" by holding up her finger — it had all been … sweet.

Lynn often wondered what it would be like to have a brother, but she had never imagined a Larch. The hand-flapping, talking by the book, not meeting her eyes — he was obviously on the spectrum, but there was something else, something outside the special-needs box.

Blossom appeared, lugging a bulging shopping bag.

Lynn jumped up and grabbed one handle. "Happy birthday!"

"Hurry. Hot doughnuts, cold milk, frozen ice cream."

As they walked through the Lingerlands toward the reservoir, Blossom started to whistle, loud, liquid and fancy.

"Is that a signal?"

"No," said Blossom. "I'm just happy."

The first thing Lynn noticed in the cottage were the flowers. Flowers and leaves, vines and branches. Not in containers but stuck everywhere, between the doors, taped to the chairs, wound around the pipes, tucked behind the pictures and into the cords of the twinkle lights, braided into Larch's hair and the collars of Artdog and Catmodicum.

"Larch did the flowers," said Blossom.

"Hey, Larch, they're beautiful. Where did you get them?"

"The flowers come from our garden. One day the visitor can go there."

Looking into a darker corner Lynn noticed, emerging from the flowery ceiling, a creature suspended by his knees from a high pipe.

Tron? Volumizing? He slowly jackknifed to a right angle, then grabbed the pipe and backflipped to the floor, landing lightly without a sound.

Lynn blinked. He was manga come to life — narrow face, shiny black hair that fell into precise points as he flipped to the vertical, strong skinny body, bronze skin.

"Hey," he said, narrowing his perfect anime eyes. "Lynn."

"Hey," croaked Lynn.

It was a relief when one of the many doors opened and a comfortably ordinary man entered, plaid shirt, beard with an edge of gray, thick eyebrows, generally grandfatherish.

He flung his arms out wide, sending several suspended bouquets of flowers flying.

"It's Lynn, the visitor! I'm Fossick. Welcome to the cottage! Welcome to Arcadia. One feast, one house, one mutual happiness."

"A-r-C-a-D-i-A," spell-chanted Larch, snapping his fingers.

To Lynn's astonishment, Fossick reached out and wrapped both her and Blossom in a giant hug. He smelled like leaves, crispy leaves in a pile.

"Did I hear a rumor of festive doughnuts and an ice-cream cake?"

"Dessert, then the story," said Larch.

The family tackled the doughnuts and cake with gusto.

"Larch knows words for doughnuts in foreign lands," said Larch. Blossom and Fossick each held up a finger.

"I know words for doughnuts in foreign lands: Kinkling, malasadas, bomboloni, zeppole, churros."

The dessert enthusiasm, however, was mild compared to their pleasure in the milk that Blossom pulled out of the grocery bag. Fossick poured mug after foaming mug and they all downed it with gusto, reminding Lynn of football fan beer drinkers. Catmodicum lapped milk out of a saucer and Artdog helped himself to a longjohn, taking it to the floor at Larch's feet to nibble on.

Lynn thought of Kas's dog, Max, and how his every bite was weighed and monitored for maximum canine health.

"Is it time?" said Larch. "Is it time for the story?" He pulled down his suit jacket sleeves and straightened his powder blue tie.

"Okay," said Fossick, shaking doughnut crumbs out of his beard. "Here we go. The day I found Blossom …"

Larch hugged himself and squeaked. Tron gave a sigh

that was borderline sarcastic. Lynn recognized that border. Lately at home she had been walking along it herself.

Fossick glanced at Tron. "… was on an ordinary day."

"No sign, no signal," said Larch.

There was a pause. Fossick raised one awning eyebrow at Tron.

"No prophesy, no portent," said Tron. His voice came out as even as toothpaste.

Fossick continued. "It wasn't even a bin day. It was a returning day. I had done with returning and I was pushing the wheelie home. I had coins in my pocket."

"Clinking," said Larch.

"Clinking in my pocket. But then, passing by a dumpster, I heard another sound. I thought it was a kitten."

There was another pause.

"I thought it was a kitten," Fossick repeated.

Tron was picking at the edge of his shoe, pulling the sole away.

"Don't wreck your shoes," said Fossick.

"Don't wreck your shoes doesn't come next," said Larch, beginning to flap again. "Tron says, 'Not a kitten.'"

"You know it. Say it yourself." Tron gave his shoe another vicious tug.

"Tron," said Fossick, putting his hand on Tron's arm. "Darken not the mirth of the feast." Tron swatted him away.

Blossom took Larch's hand. "Never mind. I'll say Tron's part."

Fossick gave Tron a steady look and then continued. "So I nearly passed by. I had enough cats to manage the mice."

"You had enough cats to love," said Larch.

"But something made me stop and open the lid. Inside, wrapped in a towel …"

"A soft yellow towel," said Blossom.

"… was a baby, a newborn baby."

A baby? Lynn looked around at the group. Did they mean that Blossom was thrown away in the garbage? That was horrible. How could they be telling the story in such a jolly way?

Then Fossick put out both arms as if to hug the air. "And the instruments which aided to expose the child were even then lost when it was found." He winked at Lynn and whispered, "Some parts of this story were written by Shakespeare."

Larch took a deep breath. "She grabbed your finger."

"She held on for dear life, as tight as a leech," said Fossick. "As tight as a leech but a good deal prettier."

Blossom took a deep breath. "Was I stinky?"

"Your head smelled like a flower," said Fossick. "So I called you Blossom."

"She wasn't a steal, she was a find," said Larch. "We do not steal. It's a rule."

"The best find of all time," said Fossick. "I said to myself, Is it useful?"

Blossom and Larch exploded into a yelling chorus. "No!

No way! No use at all! Nyet. No, no, no!" Artdog began to howl.

Larch grabbed him and squish-hugged him. "So you said to yourself ..."

"So I said to myself, Is it lovely?"

"Yes, si, hai, darn tootin', oui," Larch agreed.

Even Tron was pulled in. "Yeah, yeah, yeah."

The sound filled up the room, curling around the chairs, settling on Larch's work table, creeping around the hanging flowers, bouncing off the hanging rugs, rising to the pipes overhead. Catmodicum woke, stretched, yawned, wandered over to Lynn and snuggled into her lap before going back to sleep.

With Shakti as a mom, Lynn had been to some strange events in her life, especially before Clive. There was drum circle, welcoming the dawn at the summer solstice, mumming, a yoga wedding.

But this was something else. What it reminded her of most was church, where she sometimes went with Rob and Jean. Everybody saying the same words they always said, telling the same story over and over. Like wacky church.

The chorus of yesses wound down and Larch continued. "Useful or lovely. Finds must be one. That's a rule."

"She was indeed lovely," said Fossick. "So I brought her home."

"But I cried," said Blossom. "I needed milk. Good milk is a hard find."

"So I went to the petting zoo in the Lingerlands and

cut them a deal. I built them some fences. They gave me goats' milk."

"From the pygmy goats," said Blossom.

Larch jiggled up and down, tipping Artdog off his lap. "This is Larch's best part. Did she poop and pee and puke?"

"She did. But I fixed her up, every time. Blossom loved the milk and she grew and grew, increasing in stature and beauty. And she does still."

There was a pause, quiet except for Catmodicum's purr and Tron drumming his fingers on a pipe.

"Last question," said Blossom. Her voice was different. Deeper. "Was I a throwaway?"

Fossick put a hand on Tron's sleeve. "Tron?"

"No, you were a keepsake. The best find of all time." Tron ricocheted out of his chair. "Okay, that's it. I'm out of here."

"Hey! What about the feast?" Blossom banged her fist on the floor. Artdog jumped.

"Not hungry." Tron scooped his pack off the floor and was gone.

"Wait!" Fossick started to go after him, but the door slid shut before he had pushed himself out of his chair.

"Larch says Tron is bad," said Larch, an edge of panic in his voice.

"No," said Fossick. "Tron isn't bad. He's just silly, because look at all this glorious boughten food. All the more for us. And the visitor."

The birthday feast didn't make any sense as a meal, but

it was delicious. Fresh bread, butter that Blossom sliced like cheese, chicken on skewers, bananas and more milk, consumed in no particular order.

Larch went to one of the doors and swung it open. Inside were hundreds of cassette tapes, each with some combination of colored dots along the edge.

"Purple and green is for finding days." He chose one tape and put it into a big clunky machine. A fiddle and banjo joined the party.

"We got those all in one find," said Blossom. "Enough music for a whole life." She held a banana up to the light.

"Look. Not one bit of brown."

"Probably under-ripe," said Fossick.

"I like under-ripe."

Lynn's present, the only one in sight, was a big hit. It was passed around in its wrapped state for everyone to admire the paper and bow and the wrapping job.

"The visitor folds the edges under," said Larch. "That's good."

The bead bracelet was given the same intense enthusiastic scrutiny. Blossom modeled it on both wrists and both ankles. Fossick gave Shakespeare the final word. "What gold and jewels she is furnished with."

They ate every scrap of food. Larch fell asleep. Artdog went to stand with his head against the door.

"I'll take him," said Blossom. "Then I'll walk Lynn to the bus."

≈ ≈ ≈

THEY STROLLED through the Lingerlands, Artdog sniffing for news, Blossom softly whistling the bluegrass tunes they had been listening to.

Every time they passed a garbage can, Lynn shivered, imagining that it cradled a baby. She wanted to ask about Blossom's mother. She wanted to ask about Tron and didn't Blossom realize that he was gorgeous. She wanted to ask why Larch went to sleep all the time and Fossick quoted Shakespeare.

She didn't want to break the friendly silence.

"He would have ruined my birthday. But you were there. You made it perfect. I love my bracelet. Did you like the boughten food?"

"I did, but don't you usually buy food?"

"Only on birthdays and other treat days because fresh milk is still a hard find, and unsquishy bananas and, of course, ice cream."

"But where do you get food if you don't buy it?"

"We just go where they're throwing it away. It's one of our jobs. Sometimes they throw it away from restaurants. Sometimes they throw it away from grocery stores. Sometimes people have a tree full of plums and they want someone to pick them and take them away. Sometimes people give away food on the Freecycle, mostly coffee. There is food everywhere. You just have to know and go."

"But doesn't all that take a lot of time?"

"We have a lot of time."

"Oh." Nobody ever said they had a lot of time. People always said they were too busy.

"Where does the money come from for the boughten food and other stuff?" Lynn suddenly heard herself. What was she doing? You didn't go around asking people where they got their money. "I mean, if that's not too nosy. You can just tell me to shut up, you know."

"Why would I do that? We get some money from collecting and returning."

"You mean, like, on recycling day?"

"Yes. But mostly Larch makes the money we need for the things we can't find."

"Larch? How?"

"Did you see the toilet-paper tubes on the work table?"

"Yeah."

Artdog gave a high-pitched yip that was more like a cry.

"Oh, Artdog. Not again." Blossom sat down and pulled the dog onto her lap. She started looking over every part of his skin.

"What's wrong?"

"He has a talent for finding bees. He doesn't learn. Oh, here's the stinger. I didn't bring my pack. Have you got one of those hard plastic cards?"

"Here's my bus pass, if that helps."

"That's good. I can use my fingernail but a piece of plastic is better. There we go. Out."

"How do you know how to do that?"

"Fossick taught us. First aid is one of our subjects. Sometimes I hate it, though. When Artdog arrived he had an abscess and we had to drain it. He didn't understand that we were making it better."

Abscess. Even the word was disgusting. A picture of Max wandered into Lynn's head again. No first aid for Max. He was a regular visitor at the vet.

"He'll be fine but I should take him home and put some cool water on it. I'll leave you here."

"Okay. Happy birthday again!" The sound of whistling disappeared into the trees.

Lynn plunked into a seat on the bus. Life in the underground cottage, with a Shakespeare-spouting father, cardboard furniture, a toilet on a throne and Anime boy. She felt giddy with that much strangeness at one go.

And what was that about toilet-paper tubes?

NINE

A Wilderness Guide
to Trailing and Trapping

"HAVE YOU THOUGHT further about bringing a friend to the flash mob?"

Shakti was sitting in the kitchen, waiting for the Sunday moonlighting drywallers to turn up. Lynn was in transit from bedroom to fridge.

"Maybe."

"How about Kas or Celia?"

"I dunno. They're still in Oregon."

"Still? I didn't know the trip was going to be this long."

Lynn hadn't shared news of the choir's success. Or any news. She was working to rule as a daughter. "Yeah."

There was a clanking at the front door.

"Oh, here they are. What are your plans for the day?"

"Avoiding drywall dust."

"Good idea."

≈ ≈ ≈

DID BLOSSOM and her family really exist? Lynn experienced a wave of doubt as she glanced around before running her key across the metal screen at the edge of the reservoir. No phone. No email. No street address. Did Blossom even have a last name? For Pete's sake, it would be easier to confirm that Celia's *guinea pigs*, stars of their own YouTube movies, existed.

But, whether or not she existed, there she was, the opposite of virtual, grinning.

"The visitor!"

"Yeah," said Lynn, "and wait till you hear my idea for a fun mutual activity."

As they headed down the path, Lynn described the flash-mob plans and Blossom got it right away.

"So you're trying to change people's minds by being sneaky and you don't really know whether it'll work but you'll enjoy it anyway?"

"That's more or less it."

"But that doesn't sound like a citizen thing. It sounds like an Underlander thing."

"Well, citizens are not all the same, you know."

"I would love to do this with you but I'm not sure I'm allowed. Come on, we'll ask Fossick."

They came through the cottage door to face a forest of hanging laundry. The girls fought their way through the damp to find Fossick bent over a plastic washtub and Larch carefully rinsing out a shirt.

"The visitor returns," said Larch.

"Well met on wash day," said Fossick.

"Want to wring or hang?" asked Blossom.

"Sounds kind of violent," said Lynn. "I'll hang."

Fossick listened to the flash invitation and asked a bunch of questions.

"I applaud the idea but I don't think it's for us," he said. "You're looking for media attention, right? That's the point?"

"Pwfff," said Lynn, as a pair of pants she was trying to loop over a ceiling pipe swung back in her face.

"Well, as you've noticed, we avoid attention. That's not to say that we don't aim to make our mark. We just do it by stealth. Has Blossom told you about the traplines?"

Lynn gulped. Trapping? Animals? She had been wondering about this ever since Blossom said, "There is plenty of food." Wildlife? Squirrels? Oh, yuck. The part of her mind that knew that she herself ate dead animals was trying not to touch the part of her mind that was racing toward the dangerous cliff edge of raccoons as dinner. Were they even edible?

She ducked behind a sheet. "Not really."

Fossick laughed. "Don't worry. It doesn't involve any chewed-off limbs. Blossom. Explain. Put the visitor out of her misery. We're done with laundry anyway."

Blossom pulled a folder from under the work table.

"It all started when we found a big box of these labels, sticky but clear. We think of words. Larch copies them on the labels and we go and post them in places on the citizen trail that are a bit secret."

"But what are you trapping?" said Lynn.

"We're trapping attention," said Fossick. "Just for a second, maybe. Get people wondering, questioning. Distract them from their citizen concerns. Go on. Think of some words."

All words seemed to melt away at Lynn's approach. "I don't get it."

"Okay, how about some rules. Citizens like rules. Blossom, give us a rule starting with Never."

"Um … Never … soak your shoelaces in your tea."

"Good. Good rule for life."

Fossick scribbled on a scrap of paper and handed it to Larch. "Enough rinsing. New job for you."

Larch dried his hands carefully and went to sit down at the long table. He picked out a fine felt-tip pen and started to write on the label with tiny, precise letters.

Lynn looked over Larch's shoulder. "Wow, you are really good at lettering."

"Yes, Larch is good at that," said Larch.

Without thinking, Lynn held up a finger.

"I'm good at that."

"Your turn," said Fossick to Lynn. "How about, All somethings must report to something."

Lynn let her mind float. All visitors must report to the

office. All pets, all customers, all aliens, all people. Peoples of the ancient world. "Okay. All Hittites must report to the office. No, not the office."

"The boss," said Fossick.

"The chief aardvark," said Lynn. "All Hittites must report to the chief aardvark."

"Perfect, write it out."

They kept Larch busy copying until they had a complete sheet of labels.

"Can I do some about the casino thing?"

"Sure," said Fossick. "Whatever you like. We like a good cause."

Lynn thought for a minute or two, going over what Jean and Rob and Shakti had discussed.

"Larch, can you do a few that say, Developers do not own the earth?"

"You have to write it down. I don't write from talk."

Larch didn't read or write?

"Oh. Okay."

"Good," said Blossom. "Let's go check the traplines. We'll take bikes this time."

≈ ≈ ≈

Lynn hadn't been on a bike in a few years. She still had one out in the garage, providing a frame for spiderwebs. This loaner looked beat up, but its gears clicked neatly into place as they wheeled along.

The first stop was the coffee shop in a very skinny

building with big windows. A few tables dotted the side-walk outside.

"Sit down and blend in," said Blossom, producing a pair of to-go coffee cups from her pack. "This is your invisibility mug."

They placed their cups on the table and settled into the metal chairs.

"Okay," said Blossom, pointing at a corner of the window, half hidden by a shrub in a pot. "This one is still here."

Lynn peered behind the leaves. A tiny sign in perfect black lettering: *Best seat in the house*.

"You guys did this?"

Blossom nodded. "That was from the appreciate-where-you-are series. It might be a bit *too* hidden." She retrieved the empty coffee cups. "Come on, let's post some new ones."

Once you started to look at the city as a collection of places to post tiny signs, the possibilities were rich. They rode around posting. Blossom checked on previous posts. Some had disappeared, some had been ripped. A few had been scribbled over with the usual obscenities. Blossom picked those off.

"Cleanup."

The invisibility mugs gave them table room at a coffee shop whenever they wanted a break.

Blossom's idea of chat was sometimes almost as strange as Larch's.

"What do you think about the discovery of the Higgs boson?"

"Um … what?"

"You know, in particle physics."

"Blossom, if you don't go to school, even home school, how do you know so much?"

"I read. You can get anything from the library. Just-in-case Rainy let us use her address to get library cards. At the library you can stay and stay and you don't even need invisibility mugs. You can go there and watch things on the computer. If I don't understand things, Fossick and Tron explain them to me and I try to explain them to Larch. And I go to the university."

"You go to *university*?"

"Yes. They have these huge classes out there. You can just go and sit down. Nobody pays any attention to you. Tron does it. He showed me how."

"But don't they notice that you look kind of young?"

"Not really. Maybe they think I'm one of those child prodigies."

"What subjects are you taking?"

"Art history. That's the best. The professor shows pictures and talks about them. I tried math but it was too hard. I need to do more on my own first. Fossick loves math but I don't think it's my best thing. What's your best thing?"

"I don't think I have a best thing. I get okay marks in science, when I do my homework. But mostly school's kind of boring, except for choir and friends."

"Then why do you go?"

"I have to go. It's the law. You know what Fossick said. Citizens like rules."

"I'm sorry that you have to go to boring school," said Blossom. "Uh-oh. People are looking for places to sit. Time to go."

The day ended at a playground. Lynn posted her final rule, *No Lingering, No Loitering, No Looming,* on the underside of some kids' swings and then plunked herself down.

"What's the point of all this?"

Blossom shrugged. "It's our work."

"I know, but it's not exactly like a job at McDonald's, is it?"

Blossom moved into the next-door swing. "Fossick says that Underlanders rearrange the world. We reorder things. We collect recycling and take it back to where it is useful. We pull up weeds and put them in the compost where they turn into dirt to grow more things. And sometimes we just fancy things up."

"You mean, like graffiti?"

"Not usually. That's one kind of fancy but that kind of paint is a hard find."

"Well, plus it's illegal."

"Yes, we try not to be illegal. Although, if you walk down a shopping street there are words and pictures everywhere, trying to get you to buy things. And that's allowed. But graffiti's not allowed even though graffiti isn't trying to get you to do anything but look."

Lynn knew that there must be a good argument against this idea, but she couldn't think of it at the moment.

"Anyway, it's better when you just rearrange things. The best fancy of all is when you can get the citizens to join in. Like, have you ever noticed those little piles of stones that appear along the beach?"

"Those balancing ones? They are amazing."

"We started that."

"What?"

"A few years ago. For a few weeks, every night we went out and piled rocks. Larch was agitated, nightmares. And this is the kind of thing that he is very good at, balancing. Then one night we noticed other piles. Suddenly, they were everywhere. The citizens had started to do it themselves. That was our best one."

"That was even in the news. It went viral! It's like you're famous but anonymous. What else have you done?"

"Hydrant cozies. Floating flower chains. Those only last a day. Riddles in trees. Big picket fence piano. Beach mosaic."

"How do you think them up?"

"We just start with what we have. Enough of anything is what you need. And there is always plenty of something that somebody wants to get rid of."

"But how do you get stuff if you don't buy it?"

"Sometimes we just find it. People put good stuff out with their garbage. Mostly we use Freecycle."

"Freecycle?"

"It's where things go before they end up in the dump. It's great because you can get your hands on things before they get stinky. It's a computer thing. We go to the library and see what's on give-away. Then we think of how we can use it." Blossom was pumping to the max.

Lynn leaned back and let her hair volumize in the afternoon sun. "Can we do another one of these fancying things?"

Blossom launched herself off the swing and landed like a gymnast. "Any time! I'm going to the washroom. It's a good one here, very clean. Coming?"

"No, I'll wait."

Lynn twisted up her swing to tiptoe height. Rearranging the world? Not one of the usual career options.

TEN

A Hundred Trillion Germs

Lynn knelt on the gym floor, dipped her paintbrush and carefully filled in a large N in bright red kindergarten poster paint. The banner to welcome home the choir was nearly done.

When news of the choir's return date reached the school, Ms. Yandle had Lynn into the office again.

"There's going to be a rally. Are you okay with this?"

"Totally."

That was a lie. Celebrating the choir, that was just fine. What wasn't so fine was welcoming Kas and Celia home.

Lynn moved on to the fat S and switched to sunny yellow. What would she do when they asked about Heimlich girl? She couldn't tell them. While they had been gone she had spent all her spare time with Blossom. Monday evening they'd gone to the art history class at the university and looked at pictures of fat pink and gold angels painted on church ceilings. Tuesday the whole gang had gone to the big bottle return depot. Wednesday they'd hung out at the cottage, listening to music, eating a big find of lychee nuts and making Artdog a new spring coat. They'd biked all over the city, to places Lynn had never known existed.

How would that work when the Diode was back?

She didn't want to lie. She didn't want to abandon Blossom and the Underlanders.

She filled in the last of the S. Congratulations. Life was easier when you just texted and left stuff out.

"Beautiful!"

"Aaagh." Splodge.

"Oh, sorry. Didn't mean to startle you." Ms. Yandle leaned over the banner. "Good job. I just wanted to say how impressed I am by how generous you're being. You'll be glad to have your friends home."

Lynn nodded. Yes and no. She turned the splodge into an exclamation point.

≈ ≈ ≈

WHEN LYNN ARRIVED at the cottage, the whole crew was there, but it was nothing like the cozy party day. When Blossom opened the door she had the blotchy face of somebody who had been crying.

"Hey, Blossom. Is this a bad time for me to be here?"

"No. Come in. He's horrible. I hate him."

As soon as the white door slid open, Lynn heard the sound of yelling.

Fossick and Tron were standing face to face. Tron's hands were clenched into fists. Larch was sitting in an armchair curled up in a ball, Artdog squished next to him. Nobody said hello.

"I'm not doing it."

Fossick held up his hands, palms forward. "But, Tron, you know it can only work if everybody pulls his weight. It's your turn."

"Listen. *I don't care.* I don't care about it all working. I've got something important happening."

"Then we can talk about switching chores."

Tron spat out the words. "You don't get it. I'm sick of talking. I'm sick of you. I'm sick of this whole thing."

"Tron, son." Fossick stepped forward, one hand outstretched, and Tron lashed out, swore and crashed out the door.

There was a silence broken only by Artdog whimpering. Then there was a voice from the armchair. "Larch doesn't like those words."

Fossick went and put his hands on Larch's head. "It's okay. It's okay. He's just angry."

He looked at Blossom and raised his eyebrows.

"What about it? Can you take over Ginger for today? Larch and I will make some dinner."

"But Lynn's here. And it's not my job."

"Take Lynn with you."

The storm dissolved from Blossom's face. "Can I really?"

"Sure. Lynn's one of us now. We'll give her some work to do. Here's the key."

≈ ≈ ≈

GINGER TURNED out to be a dog — a high-stepping, elegant light-brown poodle who looked as though she would be at home on a fashion runway. Her house was also elegant, with lots of metal and wood, not one bit of clutter and a pond with giant koi.

As Blossom put on Ginger's complicated leash, she explained the arrangement.

"It's all about teeth. Larch's teeth. Teeth cost way too much money to fix. Ginger belongs to Clara. Clara's a dentist. If you need your teeth fixed and you can't pay money, Clara gets you to come and take care of Ginger when she's working. Everybody has their slot. Thursday evenings are our time. That's the day she works late. She's not the usual citizen dentist, I guess."

"Hardly."

"This is really Tron's job, but sometimes I came with him, so I know how to do it. He used to like it, before he started to be stupid. Anyway, he liked it because after walking Ginger and giving her dinner, he watches TV. Clara has the special soccer channel. And a big screen. Okay, Ginger, walk time."

Ginger angled her head like a long-necked movie star and did a small dance of anticipation.

Ginger matched Blossom and Lynn step for step, sitting down delicately at each intersection and ignoring a yappy dog on the other side of the street.

"Is this the perfect dog or what?" said Lynn.

"She was the star of the obedience school. It's like she's been to obedience university."

The leash-free park was dotted with dogs of every sort and ringed with dog owners. Blossom and Lynn found a bench.

The minute Ginger was off her leash, she streaked across the field, dodging and leaping. She hurdled right over a small squished-faced dog who looked around in confusion. She intercepted a ball, abandoning it only after getting two or three other dogs involved in the chase.

"What if she runs away?" said Lynn.

"She won't. Obedience university, remember? There might as well be a chain-link fence around the edge of the field."

An SUV pulled up behind them, and a blonde girl got out leading a golden retriever. The rest of the family followed. Dad and Mom with silver coffee mugs, son with a tennis-ball flinger, baby in a stroller. All of them were blond and very tidy.

"Look," said Lynn. "They're the same color as their dog."

"Yes," said Blossom. "Golden. Like a family in a picture book." She pulled her feet up onto the bench and swiveled to face Lynn.

"When I was little, I used to make families like that. Out of pebbles and socks and erasers. Or cut out of flyers. Mommy, Daddy, boy, girl, baby. Always the same."

"I did that, too! I used to draw them. In front of a square house with a door and two windows and a path and a curli-cue of smoke coming out of a chimney. And three clouds and a spiky sun and four tulips. Where does that stuff come from? We never had a house like that."

"I know. I wonder that, too. I never had a family like that."

"Me, neither."

Some death-wish crows landed on the ground in front of them, only to be chased away by a posse of dogs.

"I used to think citizen families were mostly like that. I mean, maybe not the four tulips, but Mommy and Daddy. But then I met you. Shakti isn't exactly Mommy, is she?"

Lynn snorted and shook her head.

"And Clive? What will happen with him? Will he stay part of your family?"

The crows reclaimed their patch of territory.

"He says he wants to. He's been emailing me from Ghana. He's a good person. Kind. But …" Lynn swallowed. "Some of the others said that, too. They said it and they meant it. But they moved on. They got busy. They found other people. So. I just don't know."

The golden retriever and Ginger galloped from one end of the field to the other, best friends forever.

"Blossom?"

"Hm."

"Do you ever think about your mother?"

"Yes. Always. Every day. This morning I was thinking about her because I'm learning about bacteria."

"Bacteria!?"

"Yes. Did you know that we have a hundred trillion micro-organisms on us but when we're in the womb we have none? As we come through the birth canal we are bathed in bacteria and most of them turn out to be very good for you. Scientists aren't sure about all this yet. We used to think bacteria were bad and we tried to kill them off. But it might be that humans are killing off too many bacteria in their bodies using antibiotics. So, I thought of her, and the things she gave me. Like bacteria."

Germs. This was not the direction that Lynn had expected for the topic of mothers.

"But aren't you mad at her, that she put you in a dumpster?"

"Of course. But do I want to be angry with her for my whole life? What's the point of that? I would rather try to think about what she gave me."

"Do you ever think about searching for her?"

"I used to think about it. I used to make up stories about it. But one day I was telling one of those stories to Tron and he said I was old enough to know the truth. We can't look for our birth families because we could get Fossick into terrible trouble. He broke the law by keeping us and making our family. The citizens say he should have given us to the social services. If he gets found out now he could get put in jail and we'd end up in foster homes." Blossom spat the words foster home like it was swearing.

"But. Our friends Jean and Rob? They sometimes have foster kids and they're really kind to them. They take them on holidays and buy them stuff."

Blossom shook her head. "It's not their family, though, is it?"

Lynn thought of the pictures on Jean and Rob's fridge. It was true. Those foster kids, they had a look. Deep-down sad. Wary.

"And besides, nobody's going to take Larch. He doesn't fit into citizen life. So that's why we can't be found out. Not just because of living in the Underland, but because they would rip our family apart. But now I feel like it's getting ripped apart anyway. You know how you told me that Tron is just being normal for a teenage boy?"

"Yeah."

Blossom was gripping the bench with white knuckles. "I've thought about it and thought about it. It can't be like that for us. Fossick said. It takes all of us to make it work, to look after Larch, to get what we need. I hate the way Tron's changing."

Lynn suddenly felt a lot older than Blossom. "But, Blossom, everybody leaves their first family. You can't stay home forever. You need to find new people when you grow up."

Blossom's voice cracked. "Why? I needed new people

and I found you. Tron should just go and find a best and perfect friend."

Lynn looked across the field. The sun had fallen low and the dogs were casting long weird shadows as they ran and grouped and regrouped.

Best and perfect friend.

Ginger loped up to the girls and nosed her leash.

"Okay," said Blossom. "Home."

ELEVEN
Dancing for Doughnuts

THE SCHOOL'S BRASS ensemble was pretty good, but they didn't know that many songs. They were on their third rendition of "Wavin' Flag" and the banner was sagging by the time the bus pulled up to the school and the choir started to emerge. Families flowed around the travelers and there was every variety of hugging. Screens were held on high to capture the moment.

When Celia appeared, there was a huge cheer, and she put her hands over her face.

Kas slipped around the edge of the crowd and found Lynn. She put the back of her hand to her forehead.

"Oh, it is *so* difficult being famous. The paparazzi! The fans! The limos!"

Lynn groaned and grinned. "Oh, shut the front door."

Kas dug into one of the shopping bags she was managing. "I've got something for you. They have such great stuff down there. Way better than here. Where is it?"

"Kassie!" Two small boys launched themselves at Kas, knocking her luggage sideways. Her parents brought up the rear, arms open.

Engulfed in hugs, Kas caught Lynn's eye and mouthed, "Later."

Lynn felt an arm slide around her waist, and there was Celia.

"Lynn, are you okay?"

"Sure. Why?"

"Well, you stopped texting. We thought you might be depressed or something, stuck here at home. It must have been so boring."

"Um, no. I'm fine. I just got ... oh, you know. School and stuff. I'm so glad you're home. And now you're a star!"

"Yes, well, I think that's about to be history. The tiger parents are concerned that I've missed ten days of school."

Lynn glanced over at Celia's parents and her little sister. Her father was taking pictures of the banner.

"Come on. They are proud as anything."

"I know." Celia rolled her eyes. "But it wouldn't be good for me to know that. Anyway, Kas and I have decided that tomorrow is totally for you. Anything you want."

Tomorrow, Saturday. She was going with Blossom to the farmers' market on the north shore. She was going to help out. Blossom had promised her a big surprise. They were meeting early.

"Um. Doesn't Kas have soccer?"

"She's going to skip."

"The thing is, I've got a thing in the morning."

"What?"

This was it. Worlds in collision. Lynn had not expected it to happen so soon. Now she had pretzel subjects with the Diode.

"Oh. You know. Shakti and all that." Lying without lying.

"Oh, boy. We really need to get an update on that situation. So, look, how about the afternoon? Think about whether you want to catch a movie or whatever."

"Why don't we get together and study? I can fill you in on all the homework you missed."

Celia's face fell. "Oh. Sure. That's probably a good idea."

"Celia! Kid-ding!"

"Oh, Lynn. You got me! As usual."

"Celia!" Mr. Inkpen was waving from a spot in front of the banner and making picture-taking gestures.

Lynn gave Celia a push. "Go on. Photo op. Inky's looking for some reflected glory."

≈ ≈ ≈

THE NEXT DAY involved an early start. Lynn had decided to ride her own bike. The Underlanders had been generous about lending their extra, but she had her own so why not use it? She had dusted it off and pumped up the tires. But Saturday morning it started making a clanking sound about halfway to the Lingerlands.

Fossick, Tron and Blossom were waiting, large cartons bungeed to carts attached to their bikes. Tron looked bored.

"I'm sorry. I'm sorry I'm late. I had to stop and blow up the tires again and — "

"Chain," said Blossom. "Let's have a look."

"Quick link," said Tron.

"Right. I've got an extra."

The bike repair was done in a flash and they set off on back roads and lanes. Lynn and Blossom rode side by side and slid into single file when they met a vehicle.

"Blossom, don't you ever sleep in?"

"Sure, but not when there's something to do."

"But it's the weekend. Weekends are sacred."

"Weekends are just a human invention. Sleep in or wake up early, it's the same every morning no matter if you call it Wednesday or Saturday."

Lynn's legs were already whining. "Well, yes, in theory."

She got a good look at Tron from behind. He never put his foot to the ground, balancing while stopped or riding tight little circles at red lights. His legs looked like some kind of machine part, and even on the level or on a down slope he never coasted. It wasn't long before he pulled way ahead.

"Sorry," puffed Lynn. "I just can't keep up."

"Nobody can keep up to Tron," said Fossick. "He's made for speed. We'll just see him there."

When they got to the final uphill grind, Lynn got slower and slower, and finally with a grunt gave up.

"I'm just not as fit as you guys."

"It's okay," said Blossom. "We'll walk."

"This old man's not giving up," said Fossick. "See you at the top."

"When I push my bike I pretend I'm exercising a horse," said Blossom.

"I used to do that, too! I so wanted a horse."

"I used to think that all citizen girls could have a horse. We used to see them riding down on the flats."

"Yeah, well, there are the citizens down on the flats and all the rest of us. Okay, that hill's over. I can ride again. Gee up, Blaze."

The market was in the parking lot of a sports arena, with one long double row of tables. The backdrop of mountains looked close enough to touch.

Lynn had always thought of the north shore as play-land, a destination for school trips, to the petting zoo in the primary grades and then later to the mountains for tubing and snowboarding, coming back on the bus wet and tired and full of stories about the best run, the best wipe-out.

Cars and trucks disgorged boxes of fruit, flats of vegetables, candles, glass cases of jewelry, jars of jam. There were a couple of frowning old ladies with pastries, a man with dips, a coffee van already in business.

Everyone seemed to know the Underlanders.

"Hey, dude. Zup?"

"Fos, old man, good to see you."

"Do you come here often?" asked Lynn.

"Just for the market and just when we've got enough makes."

"Makes?"

"You'll see. That's the surprise."

The other merchants continued to call out greetings. "What's Michelangelo got this week?"

Lynn nudged Blossom. "Who's Michelangelo?"

"They mean Larch. Sometimes they say Picasso, but mostly they say Michelangelo."

"Seventeen," said Fossick. "This is our table."

Tron unhitched the cart from his bike. "I'm out of here."

Blossom punched her palm. "Oh, come on, Tron. Stay. What do you have to do that's so important? There's going to be music later. You know."

Tron reached out and messed her hair. "You guys can take care of it. Especially now that you've got citizen support." He flashed Lynn a shiny snapshot of a smile, jumped on his bike and was gone.

"I hate that," said Blossom. "It's like he's allergic to us."

"He kind of is," said Fossick. "We make him itchy. Itchy to be somewhere else. He's obviously got something big on his plate. I guess we'll find out in the fullness of time. Meanwhile, let's unpack."

"Finally!" said Lynn. "The suspense is killing me."

Blossom slit open the first box. "Have a look."

Lynn peered in. "You've got to be kidding. Toilet-paper tubes. What?"

Blossom plucked one from the box and held it up for Lynn to look through.

"What do you see?"

It was like looking through a telescope at a miniature world. There was a lake, some trees hanging over it, little waves, a fairy dipping her toe into the water and a moon and a reflection of the moon in the water. All from paper with the most delicate of cuts.

"OMG, that's amazing. Did Larch make this?"

"He did. He only needs toilet paper tubes, paper and glue. Also toothpicks."

"And it gets better," said Fossick. "Look." He took his bike light and shone it down the tube.

The whole thing jumped into 3-D, a world of light and shadow and mystery.

"Wow. I love the way the fairy shadow falls onto the clouds. You could get lost in there. In tubeworld."

"Tubeworld!" Blossom grinned. "That's it. Exactly."

Lynn wasn't really much help with the set-up, because she could not resist looking down each tube.

"Knights jousting. The Dungeons and Dragons weirdos are going to really love that one. Monkey cage — any preschooler. Boy fishing off a pier — Grandpa's remembering the good old days. Boxing ring — WWF fans step right up. Oh. Laundromat. Save that one for me. Look how he figured out exactly the look of the man who sits staring into the dryer. How does Larch know about these places, about things like flamenco dancing?"

Fossick paused in his set-up. "He just sees pictures in magazines and books and copies them. I think that's why he's so good. He doesn't have any ideas in advance. He just sees the shapes. He really sees them."

By ten o'clock they were ready to go, with pyramids of tubes backlit by bike lights. As soon as the opening bell rang, there was a crowd around the table and it didn't let up.

Lynn found herself fizzy with the energy of it, rearranging the stock, matching customer to tube, chatting, raking in the market bucks. The sound was like a mix tape. "Amber! Amber, did you see the angel, honey? Hold Amber up so she can see the angel. No, Amber, don't touch, honey. Makes you think twice about toilet paper, eh? Let's get one for Milo's birthday. I know he said he wanted a gun. We've been through this. The other grandparents can get him a gun. Gup! Gup! Gup! Gup! Will you have more gorillas next week? Can you hold me a gorilla? Don't know how you can do this for ten bucks a pop. It must take *hours* to make them."

Out of the corner of her eye, Lynn saw a woman slipping one of the tubes into her bag.

"I can take your money for that right here, madam." Madam? When did she ever say Madam? She knew and Madam knew she knew, and when she put it back on the table with a sneer, Lynn could not resist. "Ah, changed your mind?" She loved the way she sounded half-polite and half-tough.

Blossom was impressed. "How do you know how to do this?"

"Garage sales."

"Oh, yes. Garage sales are where citizens pretend to be Underlanders."

After half an hour some dark clouds appeared.

"Oh, phooey," said Lynn. "Look at those clouds. That's the end of the nice day."

"No," said Fossick. "A cloudy day is better for us. Just look."

As the sky darkened, the light through the tubes became even more effective. The crowd oohed and ahed and laughed. Children stood on tiptoes and adults crouched down. People knocked heads as they tried to get just the right angle for viewing.

The stock lasted just over an hour, by which time the bicycle lights needed recharging, and just like the lighting at an organized play the sun came out as they closed up shop. Lynn barely managed to save the laundromat tube for herself.

"What now?" she said.

"Now we shop."

"Go with your friend," said Fossick and handed Blossom the ziplock bag of market bucks. "I am going to have coffee and catch up on the news."

Turned out that Blossom took the same approach to shopping that Lynn did. She was thorough and tireless and orderly.

They stopped at every stand. Apples, rainbow chard, filberts, fancy mushrooms, lettuce, honey, little yellow squash with necks, kale chips, jam, cheese, pink salt, chocolate cookies, woven bracelets, green onions, greeting cards made of felt, bread, scones, scarves, doughnuts and the Locavore Action Committee. Blossom chose with care, pulling market bucks out of the bag.

They bought in quantity — boxes of berries, a crate of greens, rounds of cheese, a case of jam, a big bag of bread — making several trips back to the table.

Lynn thought of those hanging wire baskets at the cottage.

"Do you have room to store all this?"

"Oh, we deliver most of it to friends on the way home. The bikes are heavier on the way back but it's downhill."

"You give it away?"

"Most of it. But first we have the best lunch. Look, here's BeanMan. Do you like hummus?"

When they ran out of money, they went back to their table. Behind it, Fossick was napping on the ground, his jacket folded into a pillow under his head.

Lynn took the chance to stare. Awake, his face was so alive, so there that she hadn't really wondered about his age. Sleeping, he looked older, but there was still a ghost of a smile on his lips, like one of those Buddha statues.

The statue came to life with a snort when Blossom bounced an apple off his stomach. They sat behind the table and dipped into the snacks.

The Underlanders had their own approach to eating, combining things every which way. Lynn had always prided herself on being brave on the food front, so she tried it all. Green onions and honey on scones turned out to be excellent. Also apples with a sprinkle of salt.

The thing that surprised her most, however, was Fossick's approach to lettuce. He bit into it as though it was a large, leafy apple. Lettuce shards flew around.

He reached into the shopping bags, searching. "Are there more of those doughnuts?"

"No," said Blossom. "All gone. Should I go get some more?"

Fossick turned over the ziplock bag and waved it in the air. "No more bucks."

Lynn felt a flicker of self-consciousness. She had been chowing down with gusto and she had money.

"Um, I think I ate the last one. I can go get some market bucks at the front there and buy some more. "

"Goodness me, no," said Fossick, lacing his hands across his stomach. "We have plenty of food here and doughnuts won't travel home very well to Larch. But thank you."

Lynn looked at the empty ziplock bag and felt the bulk of her wallet in her pocket. All morning she had felt like one of the gang and now she felt like an outsider, like a tourist to the Underland.

"Can I ask a question about, like, about money and all that? I don't want to be rude."

"Wait not upon your asking," said Fossick, sitting cross-legged on the ground.

"Do you always spend all the money you make while you're here? Don't you cash any market bucks in for real money so you can save it?"

Blossom shook her head. "No. Not usually."

Fossick tossed some dried blueberries into his mouth.

"It's better to leave money in the place you find it. Keeping it, hoarding it, transporting it — that's when it starts to cause problems."

"But what if something comes up and you need to buy something. Something you can't make or find or trade for? Like, oh, I don't know." Lynn did a quick reckoning of all the things you needed money for and came up with a blank.

"Once we figured out dentistry, there wasn't that much else. Toilet paper we need to buy, and underwear. A few bus tickets. But we have money from returns for that."

"But wouldn't it be better just to work for money? I mean, money you can use for anything. It's not like you don't work. You seem to work all the time."

"No. It wouldn't be better to work for money. The game's not worth the candle."

"What does that mean?"

"It's from card games from long ago. The chances of winning are not worth the cost of burning a candle to light the game."

"I don't get it. What's the card game and what's the candle?"

"The card game is citizen life, working for money, using

all your time and energy and creativity to earn money so that you can accumulate more and more things that you think will make you happy. Sofas and cellphones and — oh, I don't know — collector plates. Then you just throw those things away. The candle that you burn is your soul."

Lynn thought of her new boots. "But I like things. They *do* make me happy."

"Me, too," said Blossom.

Fossick looked a bit startled. "They do?"

Blossom nodded. "Sometimes." She held out her wrist. "Like my bracelet."

"But there are so many things in the world already. Did you know that there is a billion square feet of self-storage in America? That's a billion square feet of stuff that nobody is using. There are already enough things without making new ones. We can just use what we've got. Fix it and use it. All this racing around earning and shopping and saving. It's all just dancing for doughnuts."

"But I *like* donuts," said Blossom.

"Me, too," said Lynn.

Fossick put the back of his hand to his forehead. "Woe is me! Rebellion in the ranks! Getting and spending we lay waste our lives! Doughnuts are not the goal of human existence. Doughnuts are not the endpoint of evolution. Doughnuts do not give our lives meaning." With each sentence his voice got louder.

Lynn glanced sideways. Several people were standing at the table, staring.

Fossick cleared his throat and grinned. "Oh, all right. I concede. End of sermon. I like doughnuts, too. Obviously. It's human to like doughnuts. I've changed my mind. If you would like to buy us three more doughnuts, Lynn, we would enjoy that very much, especially if they are the kind with jam in them."

As she and Blossom stood in the doughnut line, Tron reappeared.

"It's on," he said. He was bouncing on his toes. "Wednesday night. Want to see something amazing, citizen girl?"

What was it about Tron that seemed to drive words away?

"Uh. Sure."

"Okay, Blossom will fill you in on the details."

"We're getting doughnuts," said Blossom. "Want one?"

"No. No refined sugar. My body is a temple." He walked away, graceful as a lion.

Blossom shook her head. "Wednesday. Wait till he tells Fossick. Come on. Doughnuts."

The market bucks kiosk was crowded. "So, fill me in on the details."

"It's going to be late. Very late. It probably won't start until after midnight, so you'll be out all night."

"Yes, but what's *it*?"

"It's more fun if you don't know."

Out all night. Shakti had been so out of it lately that it had been easy to keep her happy with vague mentions of homework, the library, school stuff and seeing a friend, all backed up with regular texts. But out all night was a different challenge.

This was getting complicated.

TWELVE
Make Like a Squirrel

WEDNESDAY MORNING. Math. Triangulation: *Triangulation is the process of determining the location of a point by measuring angles to it from known points at either end of a fixed baseline.*

Lynn rested her chin on her hands and read the definition. It must make sense to somebody. It probably was clear as crystal to Celia. Heck, it was probably clear as crystal to Blossom.

She glanced over at Kas, who was bent over her textbook.

It was great having the Diode back. They'd devoted Sunday to gossip and beauty. It was tricky keeping Blossom a secret. She'd almost tripped up a couple of times. But she could manage it.

She stared at the side of Kas's head, willing her to look up. How come that never actually worked?

Was the hum of the lights in the resource center louder than usual? Did her math text smell? She flipped to the inside of the front cover. An archeology of labels. Spiro Browning. Tartan Wong. Joe Snot ha ha. Which one of the previous mathematical geniuses had left this smell?

If you started to think about where your math text had been, you could totally gross yourself out.

She doodled a small equilateral triangle on the top of Joe Snot ha ha. Surely triangulation must have something to do with triangles.

Three points for tonight. Point number one. Evening as usual. Dinner with Shakti. Watch a little TV. Phone Kas and/or Celia to discuss Alexis's reappearance back at school this morning. "She's acting like Juliet," said Kas. Then sleepybyes under her tropical fish duvet.

Point number two. The story she had told Shakti. At Kas's house for a study intensive and sleepover and, yes, it was a school night, but they had so much to catch up on, seeing as how Lynn had missed the choir trip. Guilt, guilt.

Point number three. The real plan, the "something amazing" that Tron had promised. Connect the dots.

≈ ≈ ≈

"EIGHT, TAKE A chance." Fossick picked up an orange card. "Redistribute all property equally and stop charging rents."

Blossom reached over and grabbed the card. "You lie."

"Like a rug," said Larch.

Blossom read out the directions. "Advance to nearest railroad. Oh, look. I own it. Pay up."

Lynn threw the dice and moved her little iron three spaces. Should she buy Ventnor Avenue?

"Always buy property when you land on it," said Larch.

"Nice color and close to Waterworks," said Blossom.

"Buy it and turn it into a park," said Fossick.

Monopoly in the Underland was a long game, as each move involved plenty of discussion. That was good, because time was moving like a glacier. They had to stay awake until 2 a.m. for the "event."

Lynn passed on Ventnor. She had cash-flow problems.

Blossom landed on Park Place and began a complicated series of remortgages and private loans to swing the deal.

Lynn counted her money yet again and admired her vampire red nails. The earlier part of the evening was spent on fingers and toes. There had been a big find behind a going-out-of-business mani-pedi store, and they all went nuts with Vermillionaire and Barefoot in Barcelona, even Larch and Fossick.

After nail salon they spent time critiquing Blossom's choice of outfit for the evening. She finally decided on black leggings and a black hoodie. Lynn had broken it to her that all-black was a better citizen disguise than her private school outfit.

"Lynn?" Oh, was it her turn again already? She wasn't entirely focused on the game. A worry from the back of her mind kept creeping forward.

Shakti had been fine with the plan for a sleepover at Kas's, even on a school night. Eager, even. There was probably something up with Brandon. She was probably just as glad to be rid of her. And it wasn't as if she was doing something dangerous or bad. At least, she didn't think so.

But there was the lying thing. Like a rug.

She moved a few spaces, paid rent to Larch and glanced at her phone. There was no reason for Shakti to phone Kas's place. It was all good.

"Do you have any idea what Tron's planning?"

Blossom smiled and rearranged her cash.

"As usual, I'm the last to know," said Fossick. "Something horizontal. He's been practicing holding onto poles and pushing himself out sideways. Whatever it is, I'm just relieved that he's letting us in at all."

"Yes. He's come home again."

"Visitor's turn," said Larch.

"Oh, okay." Lynn kissed the dice. "Free parking coming up. Seven, seven, seven. Oh. Five. But where exactly are we going?"

"The grid," said Blossom.

"You mean downtown?"

"Yes. We don't go there often. There isn't much room for us. Every bit of space in the grid is spoken for. If there's a blade of grass it's a trespasser. But then Tron said that we're wrong. It's not all claimed. Not all the *air* is claimed. He said we forgot about 3-D and we should think about squirrels. Whatever that means."

"But to answer your question," said Fossick. "We've got a downtown intersection and a time. Apart from that, who knows?"

"Are we biking?" said Lynn.

"No. Transit," said Blossom. "Something about a quick getaway."

"Sounds like a bank robbery."

"I don't think he would have invited his family to a bank robbery," said Fossick. "Oh, by the way, looks like game's over. The banker just fell asleep."

He pulled a blanket over Larch.

"I would have won," said Blossom. "I was just about to triumph."

≈ ≈ ≈

THE TRAIN PLATFORM was empty and quiet. A plastic bag danced in circles on the concrete, then whooshed onto the track as the train pulled in. The car was empty as they entered but then, just at the last minute, a young man appeared and jumped through the closing doors.

"Hey," said Fossick. "That was a close call. Worth it, though, eh? Trains don't run that often at this hour."

The man paid no attention but walked to the end of the car. He had a jittery walk. He stood facing the door.

Several stations went by, cold and bright. Nobody else got on the car.

"I like your jacket," said Blossom. "The way the white fox goes all the way around it."

"Actually, it belongs to Shakti. Tron said wear dark clothes and this was the darkest jacket I could find."

"Do you always share clothes with her? That would be nice, to have another girl in the family."

"You're always welcome to share my clothes," said Fossick with a grin. "I have excellent fashion sense."

Bam, bam, bam. Lynn twisted around to look toward the end of the car. The jittery man had started to kick the door. A soft, rhythmic kick.

She twisted back and met Fossick's eye. He gave a small shrug.

Then the man yelled. It was one loud syllable, like a gunshot. What followed was a stream of words. Swear words popped out from the background of seamless ranting.

Fossick leaned forward in his seat and motioned the two girls close.

"What do you think?" he asked Blossom.

"We should get off," said Blossom.

Fossick nodded. "Next station. But don't stand up before the train stops. Stick close, Lynn."

They rushed off between the door-closing pings. Lynn caught sight of the man's glaring face as the train pulled out of the station.

Blossom headed straight to the security phone. "What's the time?"

Fossick consulted his watch. "2:17. You good to call?"

Blossom picked up the phone. Fossick put his arm around Lynn's shoulders. "You okay?"

Lynn nodded, although she wasn't exactly sure that she was. The station seemed very empty.

Blossom did not sound scared. "Yes, left the station at 2:17. Westbound. Red and gray hoodie. Agitated and ranting. No, we're fine. Bye."

Fossick sat down on the bench and waved them over.

"That was too bad. Poor guy. One of the sad and angry ones. Blossom, what else could you have done in that situation?"

"Press the silent alarm strip," said Blossom.

Fossick nodded. "And then get off?"

"Depends on where there are more people, train or station."

"Right. That would be a judgment call. Look. We're just one stop away and we've got extra time. Shall we just walk?"

Lynn didn't want to get back on the train. "Sure."

As they walked, across a deserted sports field, past humming office blocks and the open mouths of car parks, Fossick whistled. He had a loud, fancy whistling style. The mannequins in display windows looked as though they might start to dance at any minute.

"This is it," said Fossick, looking at his watch. "Right on time. What do you think? Should we buy this corner and put up some houses?"

"Always buy property when you land on it," said Lynn.

Tron materialized from behind a bus shelter. He was dressed in a tight-fitting jumpsuit thing, like an undecorated Spiderman, with a complicated harness of straps and clinking buckles.

"Good. You made it. Follow me."

Down one alley, they arrived at a steel door in the back of a tall building, one of many tall buildings, each much like the other. But this door was propped open with a chunk of wood.

"Go around to the front. Find somewhere you can see the top of the building and then look up. I will see you after."

He fist-bumped Blossom, then slid through the door. They heard him call out, "Launch minus five."

"Wait!" said Fossick.

The wood was kicked out and the door clanged shut.

Fossick shook his head. "I think I just figured it out. 3-D. Squirrels. Oh, this doesn't seem like a good decision for Tron. I don't want to see it. I have to see it." He reached out and grabbed Blossom's hand. "Just for the moment, though, I'm hanging on to you."

They found a place to stand where they could blend into the shadows and still have a good view up to the building's top. Lynn looked up and down the street. The grid seemed to be pausing, turning tide, the latecomers gone to their daytime sleeps and the earlycomers still at home, stumbling in the dark for their shoes and their coffee.

The building was made of black glass, like a hole into nothing. In front there was a large plaza. At the center was a fountain made of metal rods. A small knot of boys appeared and began to stare up into the sky, pulling out cameras. A few of them nodded at Blossom. As the tallest boy tipped his head back, his hood slipped off, revealing dreadlocks.

He turned and met Lynn's eye. It was just a split second.

"You?"

"You?"

End of silent conversation.

Two surprises. One was seeing somebody from the citizen world here. Two was realizing that Dreadlocks must have noticed her at school. Lynn was so sure that she was invisible to everyone except the safe-girl pod.

There was a little collective inhale from the crowd.

Lynn laced her fingers behind her head and looked up. At the edge of the top of the building there was a movement, a bit of scurrying. Then a small figure with a silver head appeared against the night-gray sky, a crisp paper cut-out of a body.

Lynn grew wings and flew up to stand beside him. Her stomach tilted. Was it like the high board times one hundred, or was it like nothing else?

"Look …" said Blossom, and then she gasped. The figure disappeared and then came flying off the top of the building. There was a second — an hour? — of freefall before a white rectangular parachute popped open. It seemed to hang there motionless, gently swaying. As it got closer it appeared to speed up, falling directly toward the fountain, but at the last second it slid sideways. The figure landed and somersaulted to his feet.

Fossick sank to the ground. The ghost people cheered and whooped. The jumper pulled off his helmet and turned into Tron. Everybody slapped his hands. He slipped out of his harness and the crew scurried around, gathering up lines and fabric.

"Come on," said Blossom, laughing and tugging at Fossick. "Get up. Here he comes."

Tron bounded across the plaza. "There was an eagle. Did you see it? Up there. Up there you are looking down on the birds." He jumped up and down, electric with energy, gulping air. Then he picked up Blossom and began to twirl her. He propped her up, doubled over with laughter and turned to Lynn. There was a split second's hesitation and then he scooped her up and launched her as well.

There was a memory. Somebody strong had twirled her once, long ago, before she had the words for total joy.

Lynn stopped whirling but the world kept on. Blossom caught one arm and Tron caught the other and they all leaned on one another.

"Hey!" A loud voice came from the direction of the fountain and they turned toward it. There was a flash of light.

Tron swore softly and pulled up his hood.

A beat-up Volkswagen bug came toward them across the plaza. It pulled up beside them, and a grinning, pierced Goth girl leaned out the window.

"Need a ride?"

The crew stuffed the parachute into the trunk, fist-bumped Tron and slipped away into the night.

The family piled into the car, with Fossick, Lynn and Blossom squished into the back seat.

"Seatbelts fastened, everybody?" Goth girl laughed.

"I'm good," said Tron, belting up and pulling his helmet over his hood. "Sure wouldn't want to do anything *dangerous*!"

They swerved across the plaza, around the fountain, across the sidewalk and bumped down the curb onto the street.

"I love this," said the driver. "Off-road!"

The rain began as they headed toward the Lingerlands, a mist on the windshield that accelerated into a downpour.

Goth girl dropped them at the parking lot nearest the cottage and waved goodbye. Tron ran down the path and did a backflip off the wall beside the metal door.

Inside, Larch was awake and snipping, Artdog asleep on his feet. The tale was told.

"Somebody took a picture of the three of us," said Blossom.

"Does that mean you will be famous?" said Larch.

"No," said Tron. "They don't know who we are. We'll be famous and secret both. So. What are we going to do now?"

Now? It was after 4 a.m. Lynn played it cool.

Fossick yawned.

"Fos! No yawning! Let's keep living! I know. It's perfect weather for skimming. I bet Lynn is good. Come on, everybody. You, too, Larchy."

"Larch doesn't know about that," said Larch, flapping. "This might not work well."

Blossom took his hand. "You can try or not try. You can be the audience."

"Larch can be that," said Larch.

Tron rolled a large plastic disc out from behind the work bench and they all headed out.

The rain was a deluge, hissing and bouncing, silver needles shining through the lights that ringed the reservoir, which was one flat smooth cement pad as big as a playing field. Water covered the pad, like a large shallow lake pocked with raindrops.

Glasses were impossible. Lynn took them off and stowed them in her pocket.

"Hey, ho, the wind and the rain," said Fossick.

"It's perfect," said Tron. He threw the disc across the water like skipping a stone. Then he ran after it — huge, splashing Tronstrides — and jumped onto the disc. He went skidding along, water spraying out behind him. Then he skimmed it toward Lynn.

"Run with it and jump. Don't think."

"Do it," said Blossom.

Somehow Lynn's legs knew how. She raced along on the slippery world, arms out, rain in her naked face. It felt like she could skim across the reservoir, across the Lingerlands, through the silver rain, off the edge of the world.

Tron and Blossom and Lynn took turns. Larch and Artdog were the perfect audience, applauding and barking Bravo! after each run. Fossick gave it one go and did a spectacular arm-and-leg-flailing fall. He lay on his back, proclaiming, "The roof of the chamber with golden cherubims is fretted, from this day to the ending of the world."

And then, in a second, it went from glorious to cold. They were wet through and through. Lynn felt as though her bone marrow was soggy.

Inside the cottage everyone dripped and laughed and shook themselves, following the example of Artdog.

Lynn looked at them standing in a line. Tron leaned against Fossick for balance while he peeled off his socks. His slick wet hair was as black as a crow. Fossick's beard was jeweled with raindrops. Blossom was wringing out her hair with one end of a bath towel while Larch mopped his face with the other. Artdog figure-eighted around everyone's feet, catching drops.

A family, wet and weird.

After an exchange of goodnights, Blossom and Lynn retreated through one of the doors to a cubby just big enough for one mattress. Blossom offered a selection of T-shirts in a range of colors, sizes and styles. Lynn chose a huge pink Run-for-the-Cure offering and stripped off her wet clothes.

Blossom pulled two thick knitted blankets from a shelf. They were in rainbow stripes, wild with color.

"You can use the one I made or the one Tron made."

"You know how to knit?"

"We all know. Yarn is an easy find. You just take sweaters apart. Tron makes other sweaters sometimes. Well, he used to. Mostly I just like to make blankets and scarves."

They wrapped themselves in the blankets, settled down on the mattress and reviewed everything that had happened, Catmodicum treading from one to the other with hard little feet.

Blossom sighed. "It couldn't be better. A friend here at the cottage and Tron back. I thought he might go off with Debbie."

"Debbie?"

"You know, the one with the car."

"She's called Debbie? She looks like a Raven or a Belladonna or something."

"No. She's just Debbie. She might be his girlfriend. He doesn't say anything. But, anyway, he came home with us. Maybe all he needs to be happy is to go jump off a building now and again. This is my best night ever."

There was a quiet knock at the door. It swung open and there was Larch, in a kind of nightshirt and a tie.

"Larch has a question."

"Ask away," said Blossom.

"Is the visitor going to stay here forever?"

"No. She is only here for now. This is called a sleepover. Right, Lynn?"

"Right."

"Sleep over what?"

"Sleep over night."

"Oh." The door swung closed.

Blossom turned out the light. "I wonder if Artdog could learn to skim?"

"I'll bet he could. I've seen YouTube videos of dogs skateboarding. We should go to the library and watch them. There's this funny one of a pit bull at a beach somewhere in Australia ... Blossom?"

Asleep.

Lynn punched her pillow into a good shape. The blankets were a bit scratchy so she folded herself completely inside her T-shirt. She peered into the complete darkness. Eyes opened or closed, it made no difference. She wasn't one bit tired.

Will the visitor stay forever? What if it was that easy? What if you could just invent your family, your home, your life?

Suddenly, Catmodicum oophed onto Lynn's chest and with her came a big idea, big and simple.

You could. You could call Sunday Wednesday. Be awake and living at 3 a.m. Use T-shirts instead of sheets. Eat lettuce like an apple. Blow your nose on socks.

Take four unrelated people and make a family.

THIRTEEN
Large Hadron Collider

THE NIGHT OF TWO hours' sleep caught up with Lynn in science, the last class of the day. The world seemed to lose its glue. The bracelet on her wrist, her pen, the clouds in the sky, Gabor Unger's twitchy leg sticking out in the aisle — all these things were separate, with no connection to anything else.

Her greatest desire in life, the one thing that would make her totally and completely happy, would be to slip off her glasses, put her head down on her desk and just go to sleep. Some self-delusional part of her argued that maybe nobody would notice.

Whap! Lynn's head whiplashed back. How long had she been asleep? Mr. Moran seemed to be talking about the same thing, the Large Hadron Collider. Could she lean her cheek on her hand and her elbow on her desk or could she balance her head so perfectly on her neck and she could just close her eyes and rest them …

Mr. Moran's voice seemed to be coming from far away. Another world, perhaps. "The collision of opposing particle beams …"

Sleep. Pillows, horizontality, being watched over by angels in gauzy gowns. Floating down out of the sky under a white parachute …

Blaaaaat! The torture was over, and Mr. Moran was shooing them out of the room.

The locker opened first time, the bus was waiting, the traffic was light. All the universe was in harmony to get Lynn home so that she could flake out on her bed and sleep.

She rested her face against the cool of the bus window. Bed. Sleep. Steps away.

≈ ≈ ≈

IT WAS NOT to be.

"That is my jacket. Just where have you been?"

Shakti was sitting at the kitchen table with the laptop open in front of her.

Lynn shrugged off the jacket.

"What? Sorry, I didn't think you'd mind if I borrowed it."

Shakti spun the screen toward Lynn.

"Is this you?"

There they were. The three of them, Tron flanked by Blossom and her.

They looked bad. Tron was like an angry space alien, Blossom looked like some way-too-young street kid, and Lynn looked like somebody blurry in a police line-up.

In fact, they all looked criminal.

How could they look like that, like zombies, when they had been so happy? Was there some Photoshop option called Delete Joy?

The caption said, *Unidentified base jumper minutes after his latest escapade.*

Escapade! Tron would hate that.

"It is you, isn't it?" Shakti was breathing loudly through her nose. "I recognized the jacket. It's one of a kind. And it wasn't in the closet."

Lynn nodded and clicked a link. Some streaming video called CityEye. A grainy, jumpy clip showed the descent. It was there, the glory of it.

"Was that last night?"

Lynn nodded and pressed Replay.

"So where have you been? I've just been on the phone with Kas's mother. First she'd heard of any sleepover."

Triangulation. It was over.

Lynn pulled her gaze from the leaping, bounding, flying magic boy and focused on her mother.

"I was perfectly safe. With friends."

"What friends? Do I know these friends? Sneaking off in the middle of the night? What were you thinking?"

The edge between night and morning. Why something like base jumping, which was splendid and did no harm to anyone, got you into trouble. How squirrels ran up trees. How tall buildings were human trees. How the city seemed to breathe slower in the early morning. How hav-

ing a brother would mean knowing a boy the way Blossom
knew Tron and Larch, to know a boy without all that ...
stuff. That's what I was thinking.

Lynn shrugged.

"Lynn. Talk to me. I need to know. I've been so worried
ever since I saw this news clip."

"I went downtown by subway at 2 a.m. Everything was
over by three. I went back to the friends' place, got some
sleep, had a good breakfast and was at school for choir
practice, as usual, at 8:30." Breakfast *had* been good. Toast
with hummus, oranges, olives and tea.

"But how do you know this boy? And who's the other
girl in the photo?"

"I can't tell you."

"Why not?"

"Because I promised."

The doorbell rang and Shakti left the room.

"Jean!"

There was a mumbled conversation in the front hall.
Oh, no. Shakti had called in reinforcements. This was going to be so embarrassing.

"Hi, kiddo." She kissed Lynn on the top of the head
and pulled up a chair.

"Hey, Jean. Aren't you supposed to be at work?"

"The tax problems of the Save Our Streams action
group can wait another day. First important question. Is
there coffee?"

Shakti bustled around grinding and measuring and

wafting muddled concern at Lynn like a suffocating fog.

"Nobody is more sympathetic than me about teen rebellion. I know how hard it can be to confide in adults. When I was your age I had a boyfriend that my parents …"

Blah, blah, etcetera, blah. Teen rebellion. The very words made Lynn squirm. Of course Shakti had had a bad boyfriend. Of course she would think this was about a bad boyfriend. She would be over the moon if this was about a bad boyfriend.

"Right," said Jean once she had her coffee. "You can't tell us who these people are. Fair enough. Let's see what you *can* tell us. Is Shakti right? Is this about a boyfriend?"

"No!"

"Are drugs involved?"

Why did adults, even normal ones like Jean, always think about drugs?

"No."

"Bigger than a breadbox, smaller than a house?"

"Huh?"

Jean laughed. "Sorry, I suddenly felt like we were playing Twenty Questions. Look, Lynn. You can't do this. You can't lie to your mom and stay out all night and not let her know where you are. You see that, right?"

"I guess. Yeah."

"If I've got the story right, you have promised not to divulge the identity of these people, these friends. Did you make that promise to protect them?"

"Yes."

"Are they doing something immoral?"

"No."

"Illegal?"

Living in the cottage, was that illegal? Probably. One of those crimes of being. No lingering. No loitering. No looming.

What about rescuing a baby from a dumpster?

"I'm not sure."

"Well, you were clear on the immoral question, so let's let that go. What do you think, Shakti?"

Shakti nodded.

Jean continued. "The important thing is, are you in trouble of any sort?"

It was so the opposite of trouble. "No. Well, only with you guys."

Jean smiled. "Is there more coffee? Actually, is there a cookie or something? I missed lunch."

Coffee was renewed. Cookies were found.

"Okay, gals. I've got a proposal. I think we can trust that if Lynn says she's not in trouble then she's not. She is, after all, the sanest thirteen-year-old on the planet."

Lynn's heart leapt northward. Maybe it was all just going to blow over.

"Therefore, Shakti, if you give her your word that you'll respect her secret, you can reasonably insist that she tell you her story."

Oh. Not off the hook. It had been a promise, a solemn vow. Could she expand the circle of knowing to include her mother? Maybe it could be not so much a promise broken as a promise expanded.

But then she thought of the Underlanders, the four of them backlit in their tubeworld, skimming in the rain, showing off their rainbow nails.

"I just can't."

Shakti reached across the table and put her hand on Lynn's arm.

"Was it some kind of prank, Sixer? Or a dare?"

A prank? What kind of a word was prank? The jump was not a prank. It was an act of bravery and joy. It was a work of art.

Then it came to Lynn. Shakti had no idea who she was. In Shakti's eyes she was the well-behaved, ordinary and slightly disappointing offspring of an oh-so-cool mother. She had heard her say it to Jean: "Sometimes I think she's a throwback to my mother." It was time to scrape that tone out of her voice.

"*All right*. But this is serious. You can't tell anyone. You just *can't*."

"No, no, of course not. Absolutely."

"I think it's time for me to go and look around the garden," said Jean.

Looking around the garden was Jean-code for a cigarette.

It wasn't easy to tell the story. The toffee, a concert in the rain, finding day, a boy with dandelion hair, toilet-paper art, the cottage, the Underlanders, the trapline, the underground sleepover. It just sounded so *unlikely*.

Shakti got very animated when Lynn described the cottage. She took over the story.

"Off the grid. That's wonderful. Like Pilgrim Farm up in the Kootenays. We were off the grid. It was so *empowering*. No ownership, no competition." Blah, blah, etcetera, blah.

Lynn forged on to the end. "… and then we went back to the cottage and went skim-boarding on the top of the reservoir."

When it was over, Shakti rushed on with her enthusiastic approval.

"You know, this could be the answer. The model. Small family-like pods. Gleaners. Tiny ecological footprint. Living lightly on the earth. Urban wilderness dwellers."

Lynn felt the familiar worm of worry, the worry of Shakti's enthusiasms.

What had she done?

"Shakti! Listen. If their secret gets out it could destroy their family. They trust me."

"Of course, of course. I understand. But, Lynn, from now on you have to tell me where you are. Deal?"

"Deal."

"Will you tell this Blossom that I know about her?"

"I don't know. Yes. But not right away. I have to think about it first. Shall I go get Jean?"

"Sure. No, hang on. Let's take a look at the video again, now that I know who's who."

Shakti brought up the site and together, quietly, they watched the plunging boy.

"Wow. That must get the day off to an exhilarating start, jumping off a twenty-story building."

It was like a peace offering.

"Thinking of trying it?"

Shakti smiled and punched the air. "Yes! But I guess I'd need to work up to it. Maybe tomorrow I'll jump off a can of soup. No, that might be too much. Make it a can of tuna."

Lynn retrieved Jean.

"All sorted?"

Shakti nodded. "We're good."

As Jean said her goodbyes at the door, hugs all around, something in Lynn relaxed and slid into tune.

Harmony lasted as long as it took Lynn to check her messages. There were several from Celia, saying she should phone Kas, that she should phone Kas right away, had she phoned Kas yet?

There was one message from Kas.

Whatever shit you're pulling with Shakti leave me out of it. Don't bother to reply.

FOURTEEN

Shoot End Up

"Look. It's obvious that you've found friends you like better than us." Kas slammed her locker open.

"It's not that."

"What, then? You make up some lie about staying at my place. You don't warn me. Then you turn up in some video with some mystery people and you won't tell me or Celia who they are."

"Kas, I've told you. I'm sorry about the sleepover thing. Really. There are no friends better then you. Never. On that other thing you just have to trust me."

"Trust?" Kas kicked her locker shut. "How about you trust *us* for a change?"

The rest of the day at school had a black hole in it. Whenever Lynn caught sight of Kas she was glaring. Celia looked like she was going to burst into tears.

Why were they making things so complicated just because she had a friend who was not their friend? It wasn't that she liked Blossom better. Well, at the moment she did actually like Blossom better. But that was just because Kas was being so difficult.

At the end of the day Lynn went home, checking in with Shakti as agreed in the new obedient-daughter protocol. She kicked around her room, tried to concentrate on the French skit, complained to Kapok, who understood her position completely, ate too many cookies and finally admitted that she needed to see Blossom.

"Going to the cottage," she called out as she went out the door. "Back by seven."

She encountered Blossom and Larch on the path circling the reservoir. Blossom grinned and waved, Larch smiled at the ground, and Artdog danced on his hind legs.

"You're just in time," said Blossom.

"We're going to the garden," said Larch. "Gordon is going to be there. The visitor can come."

≈ ≈ ≈

THE GARDEN WAS on an empty lot between two houses, a fenced-in area with tidy rows, compost boxes, a shed, some twig chairs. A small maple tree glowed fresh green in the corner. Base-jumping squirrels ran barber poles around its trunk.

"Look," said Larch, pointing to a pile of straw. "That's different from before."

"Who owns this?" asked Lynn.

"Nobody," said Blossom. "At least, I don't think so. Maybe Gordon does. He's the one who gets it organized. He got the people in charge to put in a tap for water and every so often he gets a load of good dirt or some seeds or plants for free. Even though he's a citizen he knows about finding and trading. Hey! Here he comes."

A motorcycle pulled up alongside the fence, and a young man in a suit dismounted and pulled off his helmet. He held up a paper bag and did a little happy dance.

"Larch! Dude! Cool tie! Get a load of this! A bulb bonanza! Blossom! Good to see you. Artdog! Handsome as always. And who's this?"

"I'm Lynn."

"Lynn!" He pointed his finger pistol style and made a *toc* noise with his tongue. "Now, you look like the kind of woman who can handle a dibber."

Gordon's device rang. He barked into it. "So. Scan the stats." He slid the device back into his pocket. "Toronto office has screwed up again. Typical! Okay, getaloada this. We got calla lilies! You up for it, Larch man?

Larch nodded. "Larch is up for it."

"Okay, this whole area here. Three bulbs deep. Plant 'em in groups."

Larch frowned. "How many is a group?"

"Oh, right. Exact as always, eh, dude! They could use you in the Toronto office. Let's say five to a group. Shoot end up." He pulled a pencil out of his briefcase. "Then a sprinkle of bone meal. It's in the shed. Then water. One

group every two pencils apart. Oh, and hey. I've got something else for you, dude. You're going to love it. Here it is."
He extracted a card from his pocket. "What do dogs say
in other languages? In Danish: vov-vov. In French: ouah-
ouah. In Japanese: kian kian. There's a bunch more here."

His pocket rang. "Okay. Gotta run. Catch you later!"
He frisbeed the card at Larch and vaulted over the fence.
The motorcycle popped into life and peeled away.

Lynn and Blossom fetched tools and bone meal from
the shed and returned to find Larch poring over the bulb
packets, staring at the pictures.

He pointed to the fancy botanical name. "What does
this say?"

Blossom sounded out the Latin. "Zantedeschia,"

"Is that their real name?"

"Yes. Are you fine if Lynn and I mulch?"

"I am fine."

Larch settled in to measure and dig, supervised by Artdog. Blossom and Lynn wielded pitchforks spreading straw.

"Did you hear that?" said Blossom. "Did you hear Larch
use I? 'I am fine.' He's doing so well. I think it's you. He
talks about you all the time. 'Does the visitor know about
earthquakes?' 'Does the visitor like grapefruit?' We try to
keep things predictable for him, but maybe he needs more
people now."

"Blossom, where did he come from?"

"From the facility. Bad things happened to him there. I
was five when Fossick found him and brought him home."

"What about Tron?"

"Runaway. He was in a citizen foster home, but you've seen how he is. It was like prison to him. He came when I was eight."

"But, how did that work? Did Fossick adopt them?"

"No, you need citizen papers for that. We just took them in."

"But, I mean, didn't anybody notice that they had disappeared? There would be records."

"When nobody cares about you, when you're a stray, it's not that hard to disappear."

A stray. Blossom talked as though she was describing a cat. How could she be so ... matter-of-fact, standing there pitching straw?

"And Fossick?"

Blossom smiled. "Ask him sometime."

They worked on in easy silence. The garden was layered with stripes of sound. At the bottom was bridge traffic, a steady hum. Above that the now-and-again creak of a crow. Then some higher, squeaky bird. Then the snarl of a siren overlaid with the back-up beep of a truck. And, on the very top, Larch singing a little chant to himself.

They finished with the straw cozies, but Larch was still planting bulbs.

"He loves anything to do with measuring," said Blossom. "Let's go pick some chard. It's down by the compost." She called across the garden. "Are you okay, Larch?"

Larch nodded.

The compost boxes were in the lower half of the garden, screened by some flowering bushes.

"Last of the winter crop," said Blossom. She pulled out a pocket knife and started harvesting.

"What's Tron doing today?"

"He and Fossick are helping someone who is building a cardboard bike."

"Is that even possible?"

"They're going to find out. Hold on. Is that Artdog? Is he growling?"

They peered around the end of the compost box.

"Oh, no."

Larch had abandoned his digging and was curled into a ball. Artdog was glued to his side, alert and growling.

Standing on the edge of the garden were three girls. Grade eleven-ish. High boots. Big bling. Smoking. Sneering. Yelling.

"So, is that like some fashion thing? Hey, Tardo, we're talking to you."

"Yeah, what's with the hair?"

"Goes with the clothes, though. Goes with the tie."

"Goes with the fat."

Blossom put her hand on Lynn's arm and whispered, "They'll get bored and go away. Don't react."

"Wanna go out with me, Tardo?"

"I think he's just shy. He just needs encouragement, don't you, Tardo? I'm very encouraging."

Larch pulled himself into a smaller ball, and the trio moved closer.

Lynn felt Blossom tense up.

"Wanna see some encouragement?" One of the three, the one with the tiny, shiny purse, reached out to touch Larch.

"No!" Blossom exploded, racing across the garden and plowing headfirst into the girl's stomach. The girl doubled over and started coughing. Her friends were squealing and squeaking, pulling out screens and tapping on them like mad.

"Get out of here! She's a maniac!"

Blossom scrambled backwards and fell, her hand to her forehead. Lynn saw blood running over the hand and ran toward her. Larch was moaning, rocking back and forth. Artdog was barking.

"There's another one! Look, she's got a knife!"

Lynn looked down. She was holding Blossom's pen knife. When had she picked that up?

The girls turned and ran.

Blossom leaned over and took off her shoe, pulled off her sock and held it balled up against her head. Then she crouched down in front of Larch.

"Nobody is going to touch you. Nobody, nobody, nobody. They've gone away. Nobody is here except me and the visitor."

Lynn felt helpless. "What can I do?"

Blossom pointed to her pack. "There's first-aid stuff in there, and get some water from the tap."

Blood was not Lynn's favorite thing. But she couldn't be a wimp in front of Blossom. Keeping her stomach in place with willpower, she cleaned up the cut on Blossom's forehead and put on a couple of Band-Aids. Larch gradually stopped rocking.

"Head wounds," said Blossom. "They always look worse than they are."

"How did you get cut, anyway?"

"Belt buckle. Fancy belt buckle."

"Should we go home?"

"No," said Blossom. "We've still got bulbs to plant. What do you say, Larch? We don't want to disappoint Gordon. Don't worry. Those girls won't come back."

"All right," said Larch.

"We'll sit right here," said Blossom. "We're not going to do any work. Just you."

"All right," said Larch.

"I think Artdog needs a treat." Blossom reached into her pocket for a biscuit.

"All right," said Larch. "Zantedeschia, three bulbs deep."

Lynn and Blossom settled down on a twig bench.

"You're right about those girls," said Lynn. "They think we're knife-wielding maniacs."

"I shouldn't have done it. I don't know what happened to me."

"Come on, they were being totally obnoxious."

"Yes, but we can't afford to retaliate. Ever. It makes us conspicuous. I should have thought of something else. I was wrong."

"You were protecting Larch."

"You don't understand. I promised Fossick. We all did. No violence."

"But sometimes you have to break a promise."

"No. If you break a promise it means you didn't really make it in the first place so it's not worth anything."

"But sometimes it's not that easy. What if things change, or keeping your promise does more harm than breaking it or, like, somebody breaks your promise for you?"

Blossom shook her head and set her mouth in a line.

"You're only as good as your word."

The twig bench started to poke into the back of Lynn's legs. She slid off onto the ground and snuggled up to Artdog.

They sat in silence until Larch announced that he had planted all the bulbs, all ninety, or you could say seven and a half dozen, or you could say eighteen groups of five.

"I'll get the tools and the chard," Lynn offered.

On the way back to the cottage they talked about the amazing base jump and skimming and how Lynn was a natural and how did Gordon keep his motorcycle that completely shiny and wouldn't it be cool if you could actually make a bike out of cardboard and how boring and pathetic the mean girls were.

But it felt as though they were just talking for the sake of Larch. Talking to keep the real questions at bay.

FIFTEEN
Zombie Power

THE NEXT MORNING was flash protest day. Jean and Rob and a couple of other faux-corporates came over early and Rob cooked a huge energy-enhancing brunch.

Seeing the kitchen alive — pancakes flipping, coffee dripping, fruit whirring in the blender, Lynn realized how empty their house had been since Clive left.

Rob said he was disappointed that none of her friends could make it.

"You know, busy with school stuff," said Lynn. And busy with not talking to her. How did it happen, that everything got so messed up, so messed up with secrets? If she told Kas and Celia about the Underlanders, it would make it better with them but way worse with Blossom. Unless she just didn't tell Blossom, but then she'd be doubling the secrets. And the fact of her telling Shakti was already getting in the way.

In the meantime, it would all have to wait until they had all saved the free world by wearing suits and pantyhose.

The idea of the protest was brilliantly simple. The protesters strolled across the bottom of the hotel driveway in ones and twos so as to block vehicle access to the hotel entrance. The entrance gleamed with marble and twinkling lights and doormen dressed like toy soldiers with braid and brass buttons.

At first Lynn couldn't tell the protesters from the real conference people, but gradually she began to see who was who. Some of the disguises were totally convincing. Lynn had to admit that Shakti pulled it off in her silver-gray suit with pearls. Others didn't work out quite so well. A scraggly beard here, an un-made-up face there, a coat from a bygone decade, several errors in footwear, wrong purse. But, on the whole, they passed.

The merry-go-round of faux-corporates worked well until taxi drivers started honking their horns and big black cars started to inch forward. Traffic backed up. For a while they let the odd car through. Then they increased the barrier.

Finally they started pausing in the middle of the road until, without any signal, they all just stopped, like a game of statues, but with suits.

One of the toy soldiers tried to make them move along. Then a security guard, not so toy-like, tried the same thing. But they just stood staring into space, not speaking to each other.

People got out of their cars and started yelling. A car edged up to Rob until its bumper touched his leg. He remained immobile, vaguely smiling into the middle distance. A zombie.

It was the power of doing nothing.

Lynn couldn't take the pressure of all the attention. There were no other young people in the group, and she felt too conspicuous. She drifted to the end of the line and found a bench. Jean caught her eye and winked.

Then the cellphone cameras started appearing, and a big-haired woman with a microphone appeared, flanked by TV cameras. At a soft signal the statues came to life. Shakti took a lipstick and mirror out of her purse and redid her mouth.

It was the perfect thing to do. It was defiant, provocative. It was a movie star thing to do.

Lynn settled in to watch. Shakti was like a magnet for the spotlight. She was good at this — a little bigger, a little brighter than ordinary people. The slash of lipstick was the exact same red as her scarf. She could have been the real thing.

At just the right moment, she spoke. "People have the right to a place to live. All people."

The statues shifted. One by one they said it. Microphone woman moved from one statue to the next.

Once the cameras were running it should have been over. The plan had been to disrupt the meeting for about half an hour to get some media attention and then just walk away. This was the balance point. The security guards and the toy soldiers stood poised. The taxis stopped honking. Everyone was taking a deep breath.

One of the security guards was the first to blink. He picked the wrong person to move along.

The moment he touched Shakti's arm, she exploded, a dry tree shooting up in flames.

Gone was the illusion. Gone was the restraint. Gone was the street theater. It was a full-out rant. Shakti's voice got harsher and higher with each word. Corporate greed, legislated poverty, government corruption — the familiar phrases washed over Lynn as she felt the sympathy, admiration and pleasure of the crowd leak away.

She caught Rob's eye. It was that look of sadness, worry and pity that Lynn was so accustomed to seeing when Shakti let herself go. And that was the look from friends. From strangers? They looked at her like she was a nut.

Shakti seemed to be winding down, when Bighair thrust her microphone up to her and asked a question. Lynn couldn't make out what it was. But she heard the answer, watched it unfold, slow and inevitable, gathering speed.

"There are people in this city who are housed like animals, in burrows in the ground."

Lynn stared at Shakti, willing her to stop. You could as soon stop an avalanche. She was like an addict, a limelight addict. There was a roaring in Lynn's ears through which she heard "reservoir," "Underlanders," "personal knowledge."

And then it was over. Bighair sped away, followed by equipment. Bob and Jean flanked Shakti, who was blinking as though she had just looked at the sun. She looked around and when she met Lynn's eyes, she seemed to wake up.

Lynn turned away and began walking.

"Lynn!"

She started to run, not caring where she went, loving the hard jolt of pavement under her leather soles, pounding out rage, disappointment and something like grief. She ran around a pocket park, across a main street, dodging a woman balancing coffee, deking around a black lab on a long leash, a crowded hotdog kiosk.

A side road parallel to a rapid transit line led to a long flight of concrete stairs, a glass-covered walkway, an underpass and an empty soccer field. Lynn slid onto a bench and doubled over to relieve a stitch in her side.

She had to get to the Underlanders to tell Blossom what had happened. She had to tell Blossom that it was not her fault.

Except it was her fault. She had told Shakti. What did she expect? She had to get to the cottage, but what exactly was she going to say?

Maybe there was a chance it would just blow over.

No. Lynn had seen the TV cameras. Maybe it would be one of those twelve-hour fizzles.

No again. A story about a family living under the reservoir was too good. Too headline. Too cute.

Lynn took a ragged breath and reached into her pocket for a tissue to wipe her eyes.

Nothing. No bus pass, no money, no cell, no tissue. And she didn't know where she was. Lynn felt a burpy bubble of panic rising.

She gazed at the eerie nuclear-green soccer field, oddly deserted. She took a deep breath and stood up.

She had hours of daylight, a good sense of direction and two feet.

It was amazing how much distance you could travel in a short time when you stopped comparing yourself to cars. Lynn remembered when she was in kindergarten asking Shakti how long a day was. Shakti answered that it was forty kilometers if you were a human and a hundred kilometers if you were a horse and one block if you were a snail and —

No! She wasn't going to let some soppy little-kid memory get in the way of her rage.

A good sense of direction was fine for birds but not foolproof when you encountered a bridge that had no pedestrian access. A lengthy backtrack left Lynn sitting by a drinking fountain in a playground, hating cars. Her heels were itchy, and she reached over to scratch them and her fingers came back red and wet. She slipped off the shoes and inspected.

The new shoes had rubbed. Blood had soaked into her socks, creeping up her ankle.

She heard Blossom's voice in her head.

"There is enough of everything. It is all useful, for what it was made for or for something else."

She looked around. The playground offered grass, trees, flowers, a zip line, a sand pit and a climbing rock.

Moss would work. Wasn't there supposed to be moss on the north sides of trees? Not here. But there were always the riches of the garbage can.

Yes, right on the top was a newspaper. She folded up an article on hockey violence and slid it behind her right heel. She assigned school closures to the other foot.

It was good. Her snugged-in feet agreed to take her the next lap.

Lynn saw the road ahead. She saw the pedestrian-activated light and she saw it turn green. She saw that she had just enough time to sprint to the road and get across it.

She didn't see the cycle path.

Ding, ding.

SIXTEEN
Arcadia Lost

THERE WAS A BRIGHT light overhead and someone with scissors. Why were they coming at her with scissors? They were cutting her sleeve. It was a good shirt.

No! Don't wreck my clothes!

Nobody was paying any attention. There was just the sound of ripping fabric.

≈ ≈ ≈

"LYNN? LYNN, wake up."

Lynn did not want to wake up. She wanted to stay floating, floating underwater but breathing with gills. Why had everyone kept this a secret? All that thrashing around and heaving your head out of the water was completely unnecessary. All that arms-and-legs business was silly when all you really needed to do was lie on your back looking up through the perfectly clear water. Like a fish, but warm.

"Lynn. Time to wake up." The voice was sweet, water bubbling over rocks.

Lynn forced her eyes open.

Somebody was there dressed in soft green. She had a purple stripe in her hair.

Doctor? Angel?

That could not be right. Doctors and angels did not have purple stripes in their hair. Or maybe angels did.

"I'm Dr. Gill. Welcome back. You had an accident but you're going to be fine. A knock on the head and we had to take some gravel out of your hands and arms, but nothing is broken."

At the mention of head and hands, Lynn's body came rushing back, or she came rushing back to her body. The exquisite fish feeling shredded away like a scrap of cloud in a gale. Tongue and throat and all the other parts of talking remembered what to do.

"What happened?"

"You were hit by a cyclist."

A cyclist. Yes. *Ding.* There was something she was supposed to remember, something to sort out, but not just yet.

She sank back into the warm and welcoming sea of air and water.

≈ ≈ ≈

WHEN LYNN WOKE for real, she was furious. The concussion holiday was over. She remembered everything.

Shakti had betrayed her, blurting out the Underlander

secrets to the TV reporter. Had it been on the news? She
had to get back there to apologize, to explain. What if the
authorities had already found the cottage? What if they had
taken Blossom and Larch away and arrested Fossick?

Lynn sat up abruptly. She had to get out. She swung
her feet over the edge of the bed. Where were her clothes?
Where were her glasses?

Shakti appeared from behind the curtain. Immediately
her story filled up the room.

"Of course you had no ID except a name tag in your
coat that said A. Smith. I was just beside myself. The police
seemed to think you might have run away and I said to
them, no, no, you don't understand, she's not that kind of
teenager and they said that sometimes parents don't know
and I said that I would know because I *was* that kind of
teenager myself and then they found out that I was a single
mother and they gave each other those *looks*. At long last
they thought to check the Emergency and you don't even
have any identifying tattoos because, as I said to the police,
she isn't that kind of teenager. That's one good thing about
tattoos. If I'm ever hit by a cyclist they'll just see the gecko
and that will be me."

The location of the gecko was something that Lynn had
long avoided thinking about.

All through this speech Shakti had kept giving Lynn
little pats on her knees or anywhere else that wasn't her
bandaged hands or arms.

"As I said, I was beside myself. When I got here you still

had a concussion and, well, I could hardly breathe and I had to do some yoga in the waiting room."

Yoga in the Emergency waiting room. Up and down dog? Sun salutation? Chanting?

"Were you on the news?"

"Yes, but …"

"Stop talking. I need to get to the reservoir right away."

"They are going to release you as soon as the doctor sees you one more time. Then we can go. Don't worry, Sixer."

"No. As soon as I get out you need to take me. And don't call me Sixer. Don't call me that ever again."

≈ ≈ ≈

"What's the closest parking lot?"

"Tennis courts."

A beeping, backing, City Works truck was blocking the entrance to the lot.

"Shall I try another entrance?"

Lynn was out of her seat belt and halfway out of the car.

"No. Forget it. It will take too long. I'll walk in from here."

"I'll be waiting in the lot."

Lynn ran across the lot, over the low fence and around the tennis courts. Her legs didn't feel completely reliable. The *pock-pock* of tennis balls, the laughter of the players, somebody yelling in Cantonese, the complaint of a crow — all the sounds were amplified. When she got to the cut-off path she stopped and tried to get her breath to even out.

What was she going to say? What was the script?

There was no script. She was just going to tell the truth. If she waited one minute longer she would lose courage.

She ran her key across the vent.

The path down to the door was muddy. It looked like a scar. The vines had been ripped down, exposing the door.

Lynn sat with her back against the door. Were they there? Were they there and they just didn't want to see her?

She slid the cover off the keypad. It would be breaking in, a further betrayal. She had to risk it. She had to know.

Most common passwords: kids' names or pet names. BLOSSOM, LARCH, TRON, ARTDOG, CATMODICUM.

Nothing.

Then she remembered Fossick's greeting on finding day, his greeting and Larch's little riff. A-r-C-a-D-i-A.

Click. The door opened to a rich, liquid darkness. Lynn reached out her fingers and let the wall guide her.

Was it colder? Was it quiet? Of course, it was always quiet.

When she got to the walldoor she didn't know what to do. Knock?

Finally, she just clicked it open.

There was nothing left. No cardboard furniture, no layers, no tubeworlds, no Vermillionaire. There was nothing but smells — apples, nail polish and glue. There was a perfect circle of light on the floor and darkness in the corners.

It was the emptiest place she had ever been, with no

objects, no people, no story, no messages, nothing to show that it had been a home.

It was as though the whole world had been her own invention.

She stood in the spotlight and tried to imagine it back into being.

SEVENTEEN

A Style for Every Story

"She's not herself."

Lynn was walking from her room to the fridge when she overheard Shakti on the phone. Usually she hated it when Shakti talked about her, but this time she didn't care. She didn't even care if Shakti was talking to Brandon. She didn't care because her mother was right.

Not herself was exactly who she was. It was like the moment when you woke up and you didn't know who you were for a split second. That split second had expanded into days. She slept and woke and Shakti changed the dressings on her hands and arms and then she slept again, in a fog of not caring.

Not being yourself made it tough to make choices. Mediterranean, Vegetarian or House Special? Bath or shower? Do the homework that Mr. Inkpen had delivered or watch videos of babies dancing gangnam style? Check messages

or ignore them? Get dressed or don't bother? Stay home or
go back to school?

Her anger at Shakti seemed to have burnt itself up, leaving beige boredom.

She wasn't even hungry. The walk to the fridge was a
matter of habit, not desire. She stuck her finger into a bowl
of spinach dip. It tasted like pureed Styrofoam.

The doorbell rang.

"Lynn! Can you get that?"

It was Celia and Kas. They looked like visitors from a
previous life.

"Come on," said Kas. "We're kidnapping you to go
shopping."

This was way too complicated. Weren't they still mad
at her?

"Oh. Hi. I don't know about going out. I don't feel that
great."

Celia stepped in. "Oh, Lynn, we're so sorry about your
accident. Maybe you have post-concussion syndrome. Are
you experiencing sensitivity to light and sound?"

"*Celia.* Stay with the program. Lynn, we're kidnapping
you. The kidnap victim doesn't have a choice. Come on."

Shakti appeared with the phone. "Half a mo. Girls!
Great to see you."

"We're kidnapping Lynn to go shopping," said Kas.

"Excellent idea. Lynn, go get my purse. You'll need
some money."

"I need to change."

"No, you don't," said Kas. "Those are perfect try-on clothes."

"Easy on, easy off," said Celia.

≈ ≈ ≈

IN A WAY IT was a relief to just surrender to Kas's plans. She had pre-scoped the mall.

"There's a new jeans store and they're having a two-for-one opening sale. Gold mine. Between the three of us we should be able to organize some multiples of two."

"What is it about jeans?" said Celia. "If they fit right they can make you feel like the person you know you really are — taller, more in charge, readier."

"Holy grail," said Kas.

They settled into three change rooms and the Diode proceeded to flip jeans over her door, model their own finds and demand viewings. Lynn listened to the judgments floating over the wall.

"Celia, those are awesome!" said Kas. "The perfect degree of skinniness."

The sales clerk joined in. "That style is so figure flattering."

"Have you got these in pink?" said Kas.

The clerk wandered off and Celia moaned. "Figure flattering! That sounds just like 'plump.' Do you think I dare do green?"

"Dare it." Kas was her usual decisive self. "Go all the way. Do pink. Remember, two for one. Lynn, come out, what have you got on?"

"Um, the black ones weren't right. I'm trying on a smaller size."

Lynn picked another selection from the pile. Kas and Celia were being so kind. She didn't deserve it. She read the brand slogans that covered the walls of the fitting room. *Stop wishing; start living. My bottoms are tops. A style for every story.*

Lynn glanced at the price tag, and a bowling ball came out of the fog and hit her.

She did the math. Three people times three days of bottles — three good days of bottles. Something was tightening around her chest, and she felt short of breath. Three people, three days and what would be left? Another pair of discarded jeans and another hunger for another pair of jeans.

What was she doing here?

There was no chair in the tiny change room. Lynn slid down the wall. Her heart seemed to have relocated inside her ears, deafening her to the pounding music of the store and the distant voices of her friends. In its place was a hole with ragged edges. She inhaled, but the air didn't seem to have any oxygen in it.

They were gone. She would never see them again. Even though the ordinary world had flowed in to fill the gap, things were so wrong.

The door opened.

Celia stood there in pink jeans. "Lynn?"

"I'm sorry."

"Let's get you out of here."

Leaving the change rooms littered with two-for-ones, the three girls stumbled back out into the mall.

"It was too hot in there," said Celia. "Do you feel dizzy? You should drink some water."

"Can we go outside?"

The nearest exit led them to a sea of parked cars.

"Come on," said Kas. "I know a place."

They skirted the edges of the mall until they came to a loading zone, then across a patch of neglected grass to a couple of beat-up benches flanked by ashtrays.

"Coffee-break zone for mall workers," said Kas.

Celia handed Lynn her water bottle. "Are you feeling better?"

Lynn nodded. It was still hard to breathe. "I'm sorry."

Kas and Celia exchanged a glance.

Celia reached into her pocket and pulled out a grubby hank of braided cotton — purple, green and magenta.

"Remember this? You need to tell us what's going on."

Celia still had her friendship bracelet from grade four? Lynn felt tears amassing at the base of her throat.

Tell them. There was no reason not to now.

Where to start?

"Remember Heimlich girl? Her real name is Blossom."

The guitar concert and the first visit to the cottage, the birthday party, traplines and tubeworlds and Clara the dentist. As the story came together, the air recovered its oxygen.

"I *never* should have told Shakti about them. They trusted me."

"You don't know," Celia said. "It might turn out for the best. Maybe they'll get some help. For Larch and that. Like, maybe Blossom could get a chance to go to school."

"School? Are you kidding me? Blossom doesn't need school. She's the smartest kid I know. She knows sign language and the names of every weed and tree and all about bacteria and how to knit and fix a bike and grow a garden and take care of her disabled brother. She can do first aid for dogs. She goes to university! She can ride her bike up steep hills. There's no way this can turn out for the best. If they get found out it's all over and it's my fault."

Lynn felt her voice rising. Was this what everyone would think of the Underlanders? That they needed help? Maybe unless you'd been there, you would assume Blossom's life was dangerous or bad.

"Oh." Celia was looking down at the friendship bracelet in her lap.

What was she doing getting mad at Celia?

"Look. Celia. Remember the Borrowers?"

"The book?"

"Yeah. Remember how they lived on what humans threw away or lost? That's what the Underlanders are like. They're smart and brave. They make do."

"I loved that book. Except it's so sad at the end when Mrs. Thingy calls the rat-catchers and the Borrowers disappear and that boy feels so bad. I cried when Miss Gilpin read that to us."

"It's like that. Like when the top gets ripped off their

world. Where are they? Did they get found out? Are they safe? Did they get to stay together?"

"Okay," said Kas. "We need answers. We obviously need to find this Blossom."

"I don't know," said Lynn. "If she decides to be invisible we won't be able to find her. Remember when we tried that before?"

"Negative thinking," said Kas. "All we had before was a kilt. This time we've got lots of leads. You spent all this time with her. You went places with them. They know people. *Somebody's* got to know where they are."

Celia took a small notebook out of her bag. "Time for a list."

By the time the list was complete, the bungee cord that had been around Lynn's chest had dissolved, and she felt hungry for the first time in a week. They relocated to the food court where everything smelled delicious. They consumed waffle fries and triple taco threats and Shangri-La smoothies and made a plan.

Step one could happen the very next day.

When Lynn arrived home, next-door Aileen was attacking the weeds in the sidewalk cracks with a blowtorch.

She bellowed over the whoosh of the flame. "Hey, Lynn! I'm going to do your front path next. Once I get this thing fired up I like to keep going."

Lynn stopped and watched the dandelions melt to black.

Her front path? Not actually. Clive's front path. Clive's front path and house and car.

Shakti was sitting at the table peering at the laptop.

"Oh, Lynn, thank goodness. Can you give me a hand here? I've got my resume all set to go but the program keeps indenting everything."

Lynn reached over and sorted it out.

"Oh, thank you, you're a genius. Jean sent me this lead on a great job in the non-profit sector. So I'm just going to send this off."

"Shakti. Where are we going to live when Clive gets back?"

Shakti took off her glasses and smiled.

"I'm not sure, but it's a wonderful opportunity to try something different, a new way of being. I mean, look at your friends. They just stepped off the track of conventional ideas about housing."

Rage whooshed up in Lynn like the blowtorch.

"*That's* your plan?" Her voice did a weird octave leap. "What a good idea. We can just take over the place under the reservoir? The place that is so *conveniently* vacant?"

"Oh, Lynn, I understand that you're angry. What happened to your friends is very upsetting."

"Shut up about what you understand. I am *not interested*. And, anyway, it didn't just *happen* to my friends. It's your *fault*. Get it?"

The words hung in the air and then started to wisp away like skywriting.

The mash-up of waffle fries and tacos started to seem like a bad idea.

Shakti ran her hands through her hair and then closed her eyes for one long moment.

"Yes, you're right. I get it. I'm sorry."

Lynn waited for the other shoe to drop. With Shakti there was always a But, and some excuse that ended up with her, somehow, being the one to feel sorry for, how upset she was, how she wasn't sleeping, how difficult it all was for her.

Any minute now she was going to start doing yoga.

"I betrayed your trust and I endangered your friends. I know."

Lynn grabbed her anger as it started to slip away.

"And I admire you for speaking your mind. You've got guts. You've always been brave. I guess you've had to be."

So. Same old leopard. But …

Lynn looked beyond her mother into the dining room. The crystals were back on the chandelier. The light caught them and danced little prisms onto the wall. It was actually quite beautiful.

Bam! Bam! There was a no-nonsense knock at the door.

Shakti stood up. "Can you make sure I've saved that?"

It was Aileen, hefting her propane tank.

"Hey, Shakti. I could do your flagstones at the back. Cremate all that moss. Waddaya say?"

"Oh. Sure," said Shakti. "That would be great, Aileen. Thanks."

She shut the door and turned back to Lynn.

"Why did I just say yes to that? I like that moss."

"You're scared of her."

"Yes! You're absolutely right. Aileen is terrifying. It's all that energetic tidiness."

"Plus the fact that she's armed with enough propane to blow up the block."

Shakti grinned. "Yes, well, there's that, too."

"Mom?"

"Yes."

"I think I'll go back to school tomorrow."

"Good choice."

Lynn headed for the stairs as the smell of burning moss drifted in the window.

EIGHTEEN
Carts of Darkness

MONDAY LUNCHTIME the program of finding Blossom clicked into gear. Finding Dreadlocks from the base jump night was as easy as plunking down in the cafeteria. There he was, across the invisible line that divided the people that you could talk to from the people that you couldn't. Dreads, ring in the eyebrow, attitude. Eating noodles.

All she had to do was go over and talk to him.

All.

"*That's* the guy?" said Kas.

"Yes, you know him?"

"Yeah, Wolf Skapski. He hangs out with my cousin Mark."

"So. I just need to go over there and talk to him. No big deal, right?"

"Right."

"It's just a simple question, right?"

"Right."

"Hey, Kas, since you know him, why don't you do it?"

"I don't know him. I've just seen him around with Mark."

"Look. I'll do it." Celia's voice was wobbly but she started to stand up.

"Oh, Celia, sit down." Lynn reached out and grabbed Celia's sleeve.

Without even planning the script, Lynn stood up and walked across the room, aware of eyes shifting toward her. How far was it? Twelve steps? Several hundred kilometers?

When she arrived at the dangerous-guy table, courtesy seemed the way to go.

"Wolf, I don't want to interrupt your lunch, but when you're done, if you have a minute, can I talk to you?"

Complete silence. She could tell from their dazed expressions that it was as though the recycling bin had suddenly begun to sing the national anthem.

Wolf said simply, "Sure."

"Thanks," said Lynn. "I'll be right outside the door."

Kas and Celia greeted her as though she had just returned from a space mission. Splash-down at Cafeteria Table #6!

"What did you say to him?"

"I asked him to meet me after lunch."

It was bold. It was hopeful. It was even fun.

But it came to nothing.

"I don't know where he is. Haven't heard anything about new jumps. I guess he just took off."

Then the cafeteria doors exploded open with the boys from the dangerous-boys table, and Wolf was carried away. Lynn watched them retreat, an amoeba-like mass of testosterone.

The following week all the strategies on Celia's list led to dead ends.

The folks at the garden hadn't seen Blossom and Larch.

The Diode went with Lynn to a Thursday night stake-out at Clara the dentist's. It was quite hard to do a stake-out on a regular city street. You couldn't just stand there in front of somebody's house.

"No wonder PI's need cars," said Kas.

There was no sign of dog or dog walker.

On Saturday Lynn and Celia went to the north shore farmers' market. No tubeworlds. No leads.

They placed another I Saw You ad and netted a bunch of replies from a whole different set of creeps.

One garbage pick-up morning, Lynn woke up to the sound of bottles clanking. She jumped out of bed and stuck her head out the window. It was an elderly Chinese woman delicately sorting through the recycling.

This wasn't their patch. It never had been.

Finally, the only lead left was a place she dreaded going to. Kas and Celia had offered to go with her to any of the locations they had figured out. But for this one Lynn knew she would have to be alone.

≈ ≈ ≈

MOST PLACES LOOKED better on a sunny day. Not the Return-It depot. Lynn stood across the street and watched the comings and goings, remembering the day she had been there with the Underlanders. It had been a dark day, a sky of big black clouds and a weirdly cold breeze, fridge-open cold. Lynn had met them at the fountain — Fossick, Tron and Blossom, each steering a grocery cart full of neatly organized bottles and cans. Fossick was proclaiming, as usual — "I never saw the heavens so dim by day."

As they paused at the top of the hill, Tron jumped on the back of his cart, gave a big push and rode it down the long slope, heading straight for a busy intersection. Lynn watched in horror, but Fossick and Blossom seemed unconcerned. At the very last minute, he stuck out one foot and braked.

"It's what they do up on the steep mountain roads," Blossom explained. "It's kind of like the Olympics. They call themselves Carts of Darkness."

As the slower party reached the bottom of the hill, it began to hail. Fossick pulled four garbage bags from a roll attached to his cart, and Tron pulled out a knife. In a second they had ponchos. Soon the hail was bouncing on the streets and popping into the ponchos. Each hailstone was a small attack. It was almost painful. Lynn's feet began to slip on the pavement, like walking on ball bearings.

"Circle the wagons," said Fossick, laughing with the craziness of it.

The hailstones popped off the plastic and pinged off the bottles. Cars stopped wherever they were on the road, the world whitened and the stones got bigger. Lynn, hiding under her poncho, couldn't see and couldn't hear. It was all about the cold smell of the wind and the small micro-attacks of hailstones.

Then, abruptly, it stopped. The cars started up and the Underlanders peered out from under their ponchos and set off again.

The depot was alive with energy. In the parking lot, carts of every sort milled, some still decorated with hailstones. Inside the warehouse, men stood at long tables accepting bottles, counting and calculating, handing out bits of paper. There was a lineup at the cash wicket.

Everybody knew the Underlanders. They called out greetings and jokes. "How's it going?" "My business is picking up every day, ha ha." A woman with hair polished like mahogany, called out, "Hey, Fossick! Not dead yet?" and laughed a raspy laugh. Blossom astonished Lynn by having a long conversation in sign language with one of the cashiers.

The people glanced at Lynn, neither friendly nor unfriendly, not very curious.

After they cashed in their bottles, they stopped off at a van at the corner of the parking lot. *Coffee: fifty cents.* Fossick offered Lynn a cup. "On us."

Lynn hated coffee. She thought it tasted like bitter mud. She didn't like coffee or coffee ice cream or mocha anything. She didn't even like the smell of coffee, which everybody else seemed to go nuts for.

But here was Fossick, newly rich and treating.

"Sure! Thanks!"

Lynn put in as much whitener and sugar as she could fit into the paper cup. She tried to sip without inhaling, which was harder than it looked. It was a struggle, but she made it, getting totally caffeine-hyped in the process.

Lynn crossed the street. That other time people had been covered in coats and garbage-bag ponchos. Now they were exposed, somehow seeming either too thin or too fat. Before, on the hail day, it seemed like a human place. This time it seemed like an animal place with everyone looking the same, shuffling and gray-faced. Even though it was dry outside, the concrete floor of the warehouse was wet, and it felt to Lynn as though the liquid was going to eat through the soles of her shoes.

The smell was breathe-through-your-mouth terrible. Not just unwashed bodies but something metallic, medicinal, almost toxic. That other time the noise seemed like the noise of work, of a factory or a big machine. Now it was just yelling and the sound of breaking glass. A couple of guys took half-hearted swipes at each other in the cash-wicket lineup. The few dogs looked mangy and mean. A young woman danced a high-stepping dance to her own internal music.

Lynn knew she stood out. She had no cart to hide behind, no Underlanders. She felt the stares of people willing her to go away.

Everything in her was pushing her to run back to the

world that threw bottles away, far from the world that collected them.

But then she saw the woman with the mahogany hair dumping soft drink cans onto a table.

Lynn walked over and took a big breath.

"Excuse me. Have you seen Fossick?"

It was as if she hadn't spoken at all. She raised her voice. "Do you know where Fossick is?"

The woman crashed the cans onto the metal table. "I hear you. I couldn't tell you."

Couldn't? Wouldn't? Didn't know? Hostility came off the woman like a chill.

A cart nudged Lynn in the bum. She spun around. A skinny guy grinned and looked her up and down. The tattoos on his arms looked like creeping mold.

"You're in the way, darlin'. What are you here for? Feeding time?"

The habit of politeness was all that Lynn had.

"Sorry."

The moldy guy gave a sharp, knowing laugh.

It was no good. The courage it had taken to come here was all used up. She was nothing here. Nobody.

She strode across the warehouse, keeping her pace just below a run, dodging carts and people. Rounding the corner at the exit her foot hit a slippery patch and she went down in a slide that probably had some fancy name in figure skating. The shoe-dissolving sludge was all over her hands. She could feel it infecting her scabs.

Get up. Get away. Just get up. Don't look at anybody. Don't make a sound.

"Hey."

She looked up. It was a woman in a wheelchair, white-haired and not one place on her face that was not a wrinkle. Bright black eyes.

"You looking for Fossick?"

Lynn nodded.

"I heard they was at Rainey's."

Lynn picked herself up. "Do you know where that is?"

"No. That's all I heard." The wheelchair began to turn.

"Thank you."

Rainey. Just-in-case Rainey. It was a start.

She saw the bus approaching half a block away. If she sprinted. If the light turned red against the bus.

She did. It did. She sank into the seat, feeling raw. To be so disliked by people you didn't even know. Anything she could have said, like, "But they're my friends," or "I'm not a citizen like that," would have been impossible, canceled out by her new-to-her clothes, her clean fingernails, her just-shampooed hair, her manners, her full stomach.

"But you don't even know me." Another thing she could not have said.

And what did that man mean by "feeding time"? It wasn't like the Return-It was a soup kitchen.

Oh.

A hot jet of embarrassment washed over Lynn. Feeding time at the zoo. Like she had gone to stare at the animals.

That was so unfair! Stupid and mean and ignorant and
… true. It had been like an animal place today, a wild place
full of creatures without names. Creatures who were not
like her.

The sun beat through the dusty bus window, too bright.
Lynn scraped at her hands with the edge of her bus transfer,
scraping away the dirt, sanding away the smell of what she
had just seen in herself.

NINETEEN

The Air Most Sweet

THREE WEEKS passed. Exams happened. Alexis continued to play the tragic heroine for all she was worth. The countdown to summer holidays began. Clive took an extension on his time in Ghana. Shakti got a second interview call for a job. City council approved the casino development.

Rainey. Rainy. Ray Ni. Reni. Renee, René. There were too many hits and too few. Just-in-case Rainey was a start that quickly became a finish.

Not everybody was on the Internet.

The beginning of the last week of school, Lynn, Celia and Kas washed up at the bottom of the school steps, stuck together with the force of afternoon inertia. An unconvincing rain was falling, and they were huddled under the roof of three umbrellas, discussing summer volunteer hours.

"Essential for our resumes," said Kas.

Celia was having mother issues.

"She won't let me volunteer anywhere dangerous or, you know, unpleasant."

Kas and Lynn weren't surprised. Celia's mother, according to Celia's daily bulletins, was very worried about drugs, cults, boys (unless they were members of a designated and supervised "youth group"), gangs, smoking, sexualized fashions (which might be anything other than a nun's habit or a burqa), abduction and the erosion of good manners. She tried to keep Celia very busy.

"I'm looking for ideas."

Lynn jumped in. "How about a preschool?"

"Are you kidding?" Celia hit her forehead with the palm of her hand. "When's the last time you were in a preschool? First of all, they are seething with disease. Second of all, all the kids are armed. Have you ever been strafed by stacking plastic doughnuts? Third of all — "

Lynn was never to know the third hazard of preschools because at that moment Blossom stepped around the corner of the school.

Lynn's whole inventory of internal organs went into freefall.

Blossom didn't bother with hello.

"Larch needs you to visit."

You're safe. Where were you? Where are you now? Are you mad at me? I'm sorry. I've missed you. Do *you* need me to visit? What happened that day?

Any of these would have been more sensible than what actually did tumble out of Lynn's mouth.

"You got your hair cut."

"Larch needs you to visit *right now*."

"Yes, of course. I'll come."

She was a few steps away when she heard Celia.

"Lynn?"

Kas and Celia were looking at her with question marks for faces.

"Oh. Sorry. This is my friend Blossom. Her brother … Look, can we talk later?"

They both nodded.

"Go," said Kas.

"Text me," said Celia.

A bus airbrake-farted, and Blossom began to run. "Come on. We can catch it."

They sprinted down the sidewalk, Lynn's pack bouncing on her back, and swung onto the bus. Blossom flashed a bus pass.

A haircut *and* a bus pass. What was going on?

There were no seats. They negotiated their way through the strap-hangers. Lynn could see how good Blossom was at disappearing. She slid through the standing crowd without touching them, like a cat slipping through a forest. Lynn's glasses fogged up. She tilted her head back to try to see Blossom, to read her.

What bus were they on, anyway? She tried to read the street signs through the double fog of her glasses and the misted bus windows. The tinny sound of headphones, a woman who smelled like an ashtray. And Blossom. Ordinary clothes. Short hair. Feather hair. Blossom who did not meet her eyes.

They got off in a neighborhood Lynn did not recognize. On the walk through the narrow maze of dead-ending streets and cut-throughs, Blossom remained silent and remote.

Questions built up in Lynn's head until she thought it would just crack open, like a watermelon dropped on a sidewalk.

She had to let one out.

"Did the reservoir people come?"

"I don't know. We left right away."

"I don't think they did. The code is still the same."

"Oh."

Maybe you could come back. Maybe it's not too late.

But she couldn't say that.

≈ ≈ ≈

THE HOUSE WAS narrow and tall, bordered by a picket fence that had been green many rainstorms and sun-bakings ago. Inside the fence was a chaos of plants coming and going, to and fro, galloping tall and crazy, collapsing and dying. There were two cats on the fence, one in each of three front windows, one in a window box, and cat shadows and mewings in the garden jungle. Several greeted Blossom and did figure eights around her ankles.

The front door opened and an old woman stepped out onto the narrow porch. She was about the size of a ten-year-old. She looked like somebody you would meet in a fairy tale, the woman at the market selling a cow or some magic beans. Her metal-gray hair was braided, wound around her head like a pastry or Princess Leia. Her clothes were in layers. Dress? Shirt? Cardigan? Shawl? Her eyes were bright and sharp. In one claw-like hand she held a cigarette, delicately, as though it might shatter. In the other, a cane.

"More people dropping in! Blossom! And a newcomer. Come along, we must all have a glass of sherry."

Lynn looked at Blossom. Sherry?

Blossom gave a small nod.

"We would like to visit but we have to study for an exam. We'll come up and see you later."

The fairy godmother's face lit with a broad smile.

"Yes, you must study very hard. Young women must not neglect the sciences. They are *fundamental*." She turned and went back inside.

A cracked concrete sidewalk led to a backyard. Lynn's first impression was of a junkyard, until it resolved itself, like an optical illusion, into a condominium development of miniature dwellings. Wooden crates piled high like blocks, some lined with blankets, some with tattered plastic door flaps. Some were shingled. Some, like leaky condos, were covered in blue tarps.

And everywhere, tails were twitching, ears flicking, long bodies stretching and eyes — amber, emerald and sapphire — judging the arrivals.

Blossom reached for a basement door.

"Blossom. Stop."

Blossom froze, her back to Lynn.

"Where are we? What are you doing here?"

Blossom turned. She looked around the garden and then up into the air where the raindrops hovered, waiting to fall. Then she pointed to a couple of plastic lawn chairs.

"All right. Wait till I get a rag."

Blossom sopped up the beaded water and they settled into the chairs, side by side like passengers on a plane. Cats nosed their feet and stretched up to the armrests.

Blossom didn't need more questions. She simply began.

"On that day …"

Whap! A cat flap in the basement door flew open, and Catmodicum flew out. Other cats scattered to the four winds, protesting. Catmodicum jumped up onto Blossom's lap.

"Tron was the one who got the news. One of the jumper guys sent him a message. Then it was time for the plan. We have always had the plan. Fossick and Tron packed all our saves. Larch was very unhappy so I just sat with him. Then Tron's friend with the truck came. The plan was always that we would go to Rainey's. Just-in-case Rainey."

As Blossom spoke, the cats came oozing back. Catmodicum peeked out of half-closed eyes and did not move.

"But Larch is miserable. He can't abide change. We've tried to make it as like to the Underland as we can, but the light comes from different places and the smells are different. He asked for you so I came to find you."

Lynn waited for more. She waited for blame or anger, questions or more of the story. Nothing.

"Okay, let's go in."

Catmodicum accompanied them.

The basement was the Underland transported, ship-shape and spare. There was the work bench, the cardboard furniture, the maps on the wall and the dandelion-haired boy curled in an armchair, eyes downcast, rocking forwards and back. He wasn't dressed in a suit and tie, but in a stained tracksuit. Artdog was glued to the side of the chair.

Lynn stood in front of him.

"Larch?"

He stopped rocking and looked up — not at Lynn but at the wall behind her.

"The visitor came."

"Oh, Larch, of course I did. I ... well, I lost track of you for a while but now I'm here."

"The toilet sucks the water down. Larch doesn't like it."

Blossom sighed. "Fossick is going to get you the other kind."

Lynn glanced at the work bench. There were no tubes.

"What new worlds have you made?"

"Larch doesn't care to make them in this place."

"That's too bad because the other day when I was on the bus I thought what a good tubeworld it would make. It made me think of you."

There was a pause. "What is on buses?"

Blossom opened her eyes wide.

Lynn thought fast. "Men and women in suits with brief-cases, baby strollers, boys with long legs like Tron sticking them into the aisles, maybe a wheelchair, maybe a suitcase, maybe an octopus."

Larch shook his head. "An octopus is silly."

Then he gave a huge jaw-cracking yawn, leaned back against the chair and fell abruptly to sleep. Catmodicum jumped up to join him.

"Come on," said Blossom.

Outside they stood silent on the cracked patio. Lynn pushed some sand into one of the cracks with the toe of her shoe.

So, was that it? They were together. They had a place to live. End of story. Blossom obviously didn't want her here. She should just leave.

There was a clanking in the side path, the sound of a slippery crash and a loud "Strewth!"

Fossick. If only she had been able to make a getaway before she had to see him.

The front half of a bike appeared, followed by Fossick carrying a large bag of cat food and kicking an equally large box.

"Lynn!"

"Larch asked for her," said Blossom. "He's asleep now."

Fossick paused. He met Lynn's eyes. "The visitor."

"I'm … I'm just going," said Lynn.

"No, wait. Wait until Larch wakes up."

He slid the cat-food bag to the ground and tried to

jump over the box but got tangled with his bike, which went crashing against the fence. "Your visit was obviously meant to be. I need four hands to help."

Blossom grabbed the box and Lynn took one end of the cat-food bag. They hefted their way up rickety back stairs and through a rusty screen door into the oddest kitchen Lynn had ever seen.

There were cat-food dishes everywhere. On the floor, on the table, on the counters, on top of the fridge, even on the stove. At every dish there was a cat.

Were these the same cats as outdoors in the kitty condos, or another whole batch? Was it even possible that there could be so many cats?

At the base of each of the bottom cupboards there was a rough, semi-circular hole.

Lynn turned to Fossick. "What's with that?"

"The cats started to scratch at the door for their cat food and Rainey just let them and they scratched right through."

"Now that you're here, can you fix them? Cupboard doors are probably an easy find."

"I could, but Rainey likes them that way. She likes not having to open her cupboard doors and what does it matter?"

"More lovely guests!" Rainey appeared from the hall. "This is how it used to be. A house full of graduate students. Now, what shall it be, sherry or tea?"

"Tea, I think," said Fossick. "I'll make a pot as soon as I stow these things away. Girls, I banish you from this place. I'll bring the tea outside."

As Lynn edged around the cat paraphernalia toward the door, Fossick put his hand on her shoulder.

"Be truly welcome hither."

The garden chairs had become occupied by several cats each. Blossom tipped them off to the tune of much complaining. She still wasn't meeting Lynn's eyes.

Lynn remembered that first meeting, sitting under the tarp at the lake, asking Blossom questions, trying to figure her out.

But everything she wondered at this moment seemed like a pretzel question.

"Who is she? Who is Rainey?"

"She's just-in-case Rainey. She always kept some things of ours in her basement. She knows Fossick from long ago when they were both professors at the university."

Lynn did a fast recalibration of Fossick.

"A professor! Get out! What did he teach? Shakespeare?"

"No. Physics."

"And what about Rainey?"

"Something called metallurgy."

"Are you going to live here now?"

"Yes. At first it was just in case. But when we arrived it was a mess here, sad and dirty. There were dead things. Rainey had fallen and hurt her leg. She wasn't eating properly and she was muddled. Sometimes she thinks she is in a lab. She needs us. She needs something called round-the-clock care. We can do that. We've never minded about clocks because of Larch. This is our work now."

Lynn scurried around in her mind for another safe question.

"Where's Tron?"

"He's in Europe."

"Europe!"

"With homeless soccer. They fixed it, those citizen soccer people, those sponsors. He's in Paris, France, Europe." Blossom seemed to unbend a little. "Fossick says that it's natural for Tron to leave and find his own home now and be his own person. But I still hate it."

Lynn fished around for something comforting to say. While she fished, Blossom retreated again. "He left a few days after we ... moved."

Tron, not such a safe subject after all. The jump, the photo, the protest, the accident. There was nothing left for a real question that could avoid that string of events. There was nothing left but silence. Silence and the distant whistling of a teakettle.

She had to reach Blossom before Fossick and Rainey appeared.

"Blossom?"

Blossom finally met her eyes. She had a direct gaze like a baby or an animal.

"I'm sorry."

Blossom did not say, "It's all right" or "No problem."

A heavy cat jumped into Lynn's lap. She gasped. It had huge paws with ... six toes. It began to knead her leg, purring with the sound of a small lawn mower. Blossom con-

tinued to stare at Lynn, and something changed behind her
eyes. The purring increased in volume, the lawn mower hit
a patch of thick damp grass, and Lynn felt sharp claws just
about to pierce her jeans.

It didn't quite hurt, not yet.

Blossom gave a small nod and a smaller smile, and there
was a slight shimmer as the world righted itself.

The six-toed cat, sensing a shift in the universe, cele-
brated by digging its claws right through the denim and
into Lynn's leg.

"Yow!" Lynn tipped him off her lap and rubbed at the
wounds. "Which one was that?"

"Florio."

"Do they all have names?"

"Just Mister Mister, Flex, Thomas, Peka, Ginger, Ptah,
Coco, Smollet, Yoda, Spork, Harriet, Phoebe, Louis, Ein-
stein, Miaow-Man, Moneypenny, Lady Jane Grey, Nim-
bus, Zoe, Sebastian, Lydia, Bob, Dorian, Ginger, Sasha and
Kootenay."

"How did she get so many?"

"She said that after five or so there's no reason to ever
say no to a cat again."

"Wow. She must seriously like cats."

"Actually she says that she would much prefer a dog.
She's delighted to have Artdog here. When she was working at the lab she just got a cat as a placeholder until she
could stay home with a dog."

"She prefers dogs?"

Blossom nodded.

"She has seventeen or maybe it is twenty-four cats and she prefers dogs?"

Blossom nodded again.

"Blossom?"

"Hm?"

"That is absolutely and totally one hundred percent crazy."

Blossom's microsmile spread across her face like cartoon fire, running up a fuse toward a stick of TNT and exploding with a grin, a hiccup and then a full-on, no-holds-barred, nose-running belly laugh.

Lynn was one short step behind.

And then it was one great huge tumble of laughter — at too many cats, at citizen world, at the surprise of a friendship that hit an iceberg but was saved before it sank, laughter at laughter itself.

Fossick and Rainey appeared, balancing cups and plates and a teapot, backing through the screen door. As they made their way precariously down the steps, the basement door opened as well. Larch took one tentative step into the yard, a boy in a baggy blue fleece with a red silk tie neatly knotted around his neck.

"Larch!" said Rainey. "Come join us. We are, it seems, having a party."

Larch shook his head. "It is not the right outside."

Fossick gestured grandly from the steps, endangering the teapot. "The climate's delicate, the air most sweet, fertile the isle, the temple much surpassing the common praise it bears. Catmodicum and Artdog have braved the out of doors. Perhaps you will tomorrow."

"Will the visitor come again?"

Yes or no. Larch always needed yes or no, nothing in between.

Lynn glanced at Blossom. This was her question to answer.

Blossom tilted her head and appeared to consider.

Cats shifted. Everything shifted.

Then she grinned. "Yes, she will."

About the Author

SARAH ELLIS is the author of sixteen books for young readers, including *The Baby Project* and *Odd Man Out*. She has won the Mr. Christie's Book Award, the Violet Downey Book Award, the Governor General's Award, the Sheila A. Egoff Children's Literature Prize and the TD Canadian Children's Literature Award. Her books have been translated into French, Spanish, Danish, Chinese and Japanese. She is a masthead reviewer for the *Horn Book Magazine* and was recently writer-in-residence at the Toronto Public Library.

In 2013 Sarah was nominated for the prestigious Astrid Lindgren Memorial Award, children's literature's richest prize. She was also honored with the 2013 Lieutenant Governor's Award for Literary Excellence.

Sarah teaches in the MFA program at Vermont College of Fine Arts. She lives in Vancouver.